REBEL ⟁ FORCE

Trapped

Trapped

Hostage

Renegade

Firefight

Trapped

Uprising

Trapped

BY ALEX WHEELER

SCHOLASTIC INC.

New York Toronto London Auckland Sydney Mexico City New Delhi Hong Kong

www.starwars.com
www.scholastic.com

ISBN: 978-0-545-14085-0

12 11 10 9 8 7 6 5 4 3 2 1   10 11 12 13/0

Book design by Rick DeMonico
Cover illustrations by Randy Martinez
Printed in the U.S.A.   40
First printing, January 2010

Trapped

Trapped

*T*he prisoner refuses to cooperate. He leans back in his chair, smiles at his interrogator, lips sealed, confident that he will win out, that his will is indomitable. He is stubborn, cocky, defiant.

He is wrong.

Luke Skywalker sits down across from the prisoner, aiming a fierce, steady gaze at the man. "You will tell me what I need to know," Luke says in a low voice.

The prisoner shakes his head. But he is no match for Luke. No match for the power of a Jedi.

Luke clears his mind of distractions, focuses on the prisoner, on the answers he needs and the steely mind that contains them. "You will tell me what I need to know," he says again.

Dazed, the prisoner nods. "I will tell you what you need to know."

For so long, he has tried so hard — tried to connect to

the Force, tried to bend it to his will, never understanding the true lesson of the Jedi.

Luke allows the Force to flow through him. It binds him to this man, to this cell, to everything and everyone in the galaxy. And now that he understands this, he can do anything. "You will tell me the name of your employer and where to find him," Luke says.

The prisoner nods again. "I will tell you the name of my employer and where to find him," he agrees. The Force twists his mind, draws the words out of him. "His name is—"

"Luke!"

Luke's eyes popped open. A sharp rapping at the door kept him from dropping back to sleep. He'd been dreaming about . . . well, *something*. *Something important*, he thought, the memory licking at the corners of his mind. But as he tried to reach for it, the door flew open, and Han Solo blew into the room. The last traces of the dream evaporated, like dew in the morning sun.

"Sweet dreams, kid?" Han asked with a mocking grin.

Luke just groaned, glancing at the clock. It was a little past four in the morning. He'd gone to sleep only a few hours before, after a long, frustrating evening of questioning their prisoner.

Prisoner. Luke winced at the word. The *prisoner* had saved Luke's life on Kamino, more than once. He'd proven himself brave and honorable, a man of his word. He'd fought off a sea monster, shot down Imperial fighters, and wielded Luke's lightsaber with more speed and grace than Luke could ever hope to achieve. Yet he'd refused to say where he had learned to fight with the Jedi weapon. Just as he'd refused to admit who had sent him to Kamino — who had hired him to follow the Rebels and shoot Luke Skywalker out of the sky.

He'd refused to give them anything but his name: Lune Divinian.

A stranger, a paid assassin, the key to tracking down the man determined to see Luke dead . . . and yet, after Kamino, Luke couldn't help thinking of Div as a friend.

He climbed out of bed, shrugging off his doubts. Not long ago, he had befriended a mysterious stranger, a man who had also seemed brave and honorable, who had saved his life. And trusting the wrong man had almost killed him. Lesson learned: Trust could be dangerous. Unearned trust could be fatal.

"What do you want, Han?" Luke asked wearily. "It's practically the middle of the night."

"Hey, if you'd rather nap, we can tuck you back into your cradle and —"

"Han!" Luke snapped. "What is it?"

"Nothing much," Han said lightly. "Just thought you might want to know, our prisoner's asking for you. Says he's ready to make a deal."

• • •

"I'm here. What's the deal?" Luke asked. Div was locked in the brig, where he'd been since they had returned from Kamino a week before. The small cell wasn't that much barer than Luke's own room; like that sparse chamber, it had a thin mattress, a table, a chair, and little else. Luke could almost imagine he was in the Rebel barracks — if he ignored the lack of windows.

And the locked door.

Luke hated seeing Div like this, penned up like an animal.

Div kicked his legs up onto the flimsy mattress. He stretched out like he was lying on an Amfarian beach, luxuriating under the red sun. "The deal is, you let me go. Now. Or I escape and tell the Empire everything there is to know about this place, and your little alliance." He clapped his hands together once, loudly. "End of the Rebellion, just like that."

"You wouldn't do that," Luke said. He didn't know why, but he was sure it was true.

"Wouldn't I?"

They glared at each other. Luke looked away first. *This is the right thing*, he told himself. *It's our only choice.* But it didn't ring true. Yes, Div had valuable information. Yes, he'd proven himself an enemy of the Rebellion. But he'd had plenty of chances to kill Luke. He hadn't.

And the anger on his face when they'd accused him of working for the Empire — that had been real.

"You knew we'd never agree to those terms," Luke said.

"Maybe."

"So why drag me out here in the middle of the night?" Luke asked, irritated.

Div slapped the worn mattress. "Couldn't sleep. So why should you?"

If it hadn't been the middle of the night, Luke might have laughed. "You don't need to make any deals," he said instead. They'd been over this ground before. "Just tell us what we want to know. The name of your employer, and where to find him. That's all. Then you can leave here to go do . . . whatever it is you do."

"You want me to talk, you're going to have to make me." Div didn't look too worried. Surely he knew that the Rebel Alliance wasn't like the Empire, that they would never resort to torture or interrogation droids. Or maybe he was just certain that no matter what happened he'd keep his secrets to himself.

Luke drummed his fingers against the hilt of his lightsaber. "What if I *could* make you?" he said slowly. "You're forgetting, I'm a Jedi."

"You have a lightsaber," Div said. "It doesn't make you a Jedi. Trust me."

"The Force can have a strong influence on the weak-minded."

"You think I have a weak mind?" Div grinned. "Go ahead. Try me."

If only he could. Luke could feel the power within him. Why couldn't he access it? No matter how hard he pushed himself, how hard he tried to connect with the Force, it eluded his grasp. His failure was more frustrating than ever. He felt like the solution was fluttering at the edges of his memory, like a half-remembered dream. But that was silly. He didn't know how to use the Force, had never known. Because Ben had died before he could teach Luke all he needed to know.

He felt a surge of anger at the thought of Darth Vader and his red lightsaber slicing through Obi-Wan's body like it was made of air.

"This is useless," he said, fury boiling beneath his words.

"Like I've been telling you."

The anger is your true enemy. The words just popped into his head. They made little sense, but he felt they were true.

"I'm leaving," he said abruptly. The longer he stayed and the angrier he got, the bigger the chance he'd do something he would regret.

"Not so easy, this Jedi stuff, is it?" Div asked as Luke stepped out of the cell. He muttered something else under his breath, something Luke didn't quite catch. But it sounded almost like *I should know.*

In a dark corner of space, just beyond the Rebel defenses, a ship waited.

And inside the ship, three men.

Biding their time.

They had no names, not anymore. This was how the Dark Lord had wanted it. They no longer needed their own identities. They were servants of the Empire, nothing more. And they were on a mission.

At their signal, a fleet of TIE fighters swooped into the moon's thick atmosphere and opened fire on the Rebel scum. The sky lit with explosions and laserfire. Flaming shrapnel screamed through the clouds. The Rebels scrambled a squadron of X-wings, but the pathetic ships would be no match for the Imperial attack.

And if they were: No matter.

The attack was merely a distraction, a decoy.

Something to occupy the Rebels while a single, stealthy Imperial ship slid into the atmosphere and streaked toward the jungle. With the fireworks of battle blasting above, no one would notice the grey bullet of a ship or its slim trail of exhaust. No one would realize that the perimeter had been breached. No one would understand why, without warning or reason, the TIE fighters suddenly turned and fled.

No one would stop the three men from carrying out their dark mission.

You will bring it to me, Lord Vader had commanded them. *Do not fail.*

They didn't intend to.

Div stretched out, struggling to get comfortable. At least they'd given him a mattress, so he didn't have to sleep on the floor. In fact, there was little to complain about. The room the Rebels had locked him in was relatively clean, with no borrats nibbling at his toes as he slept. He was alone, safe from the snoring or sneak attacks of a hostile roommate. Food appeared regularly and was usually warm, sometimes even edible. As cells went, this one was nearly pleasant.

But it was still a cell.

It was still four walls and a locked door, caging him inside. And so it was still intolerable.

Div closed his eyes, drawing in slow, even breaths. It was important to sleep when he could. He had to stay sharp so that when his chance for escape came, he could seize it.

Breaking out of a Rebel jail cell, Div thought wryly. *Wonder what Trever would think of that.*

But he didn't have to wonder; he knew. His adopted brother would have been ashamed that Div had ended up there in the first place. No, not ashamed. Disgusted.

Hired by an Imperial agent to kill a key member of the resistance? If Trever were here, he probably would have been the first to throw Div into a cell.

Except that I have no proof that he was an Imperial agent, Div told himself. Although he'd had his suspicions — and ignored them.

And I wasn't hired to kill Luke. I was hired to face him in a fair fight, pilot to pilot, may the best man win, Div thought. Even though the "fair fight" had been an ambush.

Trever can't judge me anymore, Div told himself. *He's dead.*

He had no answer to that. Trever was dead, just like everyone else he'd ever cared about. That was where standing up to the Empire landed you. If Div hadn't wised up, he'd be in an *Imperial* cell right then. And the Imperials didn't give you mattresses or hot food or showers. They gave you interrogation droids and firing squads.

Div also told himself that he had good reasons for refusing to answer Luke's questions. Divulging information about an employer — no matter how little he had — was bad for business. But a small buried part of him knew that that cold, dangerous man had been an Imperial. And that if Div helped the Rebels track him down, there would be no mercy.

Trever would want me to survive, Div thought. *No matter what it took.*

He wasn't sure it was true. But Trever wasn't around to argue.

Div sat up. He'd heard something.

No, that wasn't quite right. He'd *felt* something. It was a not-quite-right feeling, like an icy puff of air against the back of his neck. Trusting his instincts, he leapt to his feet. As a child, he'd had a fine-tuned radar for impending danger. His Jedi teachers, Ry-Gaul and Garen Muln, had shown him how to detect disturbances in the Force, tiny fluctuations that meant darkness was near. Those skills were gone now, along with Ry-Gaul and Garen Muln, along with the boy he'd been, the one everyone thought could become a Jedi. But he still knew when it was time to run. Not that he could run, not through a locked durasteel door. But he jumped to his feet, assuming a fighting stance. When trouble showed its face, he would be ready.

But there were some things you couldn't fight.

A thick yellow gas wafted into the cell from beneath the door. Div pressed his shirt over his nose and mouth, taking quick, shallow breaths. The room filled with the gas. There was nowhere to hide and nothing he could do but inhale the foul, acrid smoke.

A fog swept across his brain, making him woozy. *Stay alert,* he ordered himself, wobbling on his feet. Red spots swam in front of his eyes. His limbs grew heavy, and his head lolled on his shoulders. *Must . . . not . . . breathe,* he thought, leaning against the wall, fighting to stay upright.

But as the gas burned his throat and lungs, his legs gave out beneath him. He slid to the floor, helpless.

An explosion shook the cell, and the door blew inward.

Fight, Div told himself. Two masked men stepped into the cell. *Run. Escape.*

But the fog filling his mind had turned to a thick, soupy black. As the masked men approached, his eyes slipped shut. His body went limp. His thoughts drifted away.

Div drifted away.

irens blared across the Rebel Base. Luke, Leia, and Han raced toward Div's cell. The door had been torn from its hinges. Han looked inside, preparing himself for the worst. But the cell was empty. Div was gone. "How'd he manage that?" Han wondered.

Behind him, R2-D2, Luke's little astromech droid, beeped urgently.

"Captain Solo, he says he's tapped into the security holocam feed," C-3PO, R2-D2's protocol droid counterpart, reported. "The prisoner didn't escape. He was kidnapped!"

"We need to meet with General Rieekan and decide how to proceed," Leia said in alarm.

Han looked at her like she was crazy. "You meet with whoever you want, honey," he told her. "I'm going to find our missing prisoner."

They were all certain that Div was working for X-7, an Imperial assassin determined to murder Luke. Hiring Div wasn't X-7's first attempt. He'd tried to kill Luke several times — and had once set up *Han* to look like the assassin. It wasn't the kind of thing Han was ready to forget. X-7 was due for some payback. And he had disappeared. Div might be their only way of finding him.

Besides, even if Div was a hired gun for an Imperial assassin, he'd turned out to be a pretty good guy. He'd helped Han out of more than one tight situation, and Han wasn't about to let a bunch of kidnappers just carry him off into the jungle. Not without a fight.

"We need a strategy, Han!" Leia said, looking annoyed. Of course, she rarely looked any other way — at least, when she was looking at him. "We can't go rushing into the jungle without any —"

Ignoring her, Han cocked his head at Luke. "You coming, kid?"

Luke glanced back and forth between Han and Leia. He hesitated for only a second. "We can't waste time," he told Leia apologetically. "If we lose Div, we'll never find X-7."

Han stole a moment to shoot Leia a victorious look. Then he took off toward the exit. He hoped that once they got outside, they could spot signs of a struggle or *something* to lead them in the right direction. Without pausing, he activated his comlink. "Chewie, we've got a situation here. Meet me at the barracks, quick as you can."

Behind him, he heard Leia ordering C-3PO to report to General Rieekan. Then she said, "Come on, Artoo. Looks like it's up to us to keep Han out of trouble."

Han grinned. *Good luck, lady,* he thought.

It was a fool's mission. But it was always fun to watch her try.

They trooped through the trees, following a twisting path of broken branches and shallow footprints. The trail ended in a narrow clearing at the heart of the jungle. R2-D2's tracking skills had led them this far. But now he was picking up no traces of Div anywhere. Chewbacca, who had a much keener sense of smell than the humans, was also having no luck. They'd reached a dead end.

"No, we are *not* turning back," Luke insisted angrily.

"What else can we do?" Leia asked.

"*Find him,*" Luke said. "This is our fault."

Leia shook her head. "Luke, no —"

"*We* locked him up," Luke said. "*We* bound him. And when they came for him . . ." He shook his head. "We have to find him."

"You ever think he might not want to be found?"

Han said. "Maybe this whole thing's a setup. Some of his friends bust him out, make it look like a kidnapping —"

"No," Luke retorted. "Div wouldn't —" He cut himself off. "Okay. Maybe you're right."

Leia looked at him in surprise. She knew that Luke had come to trust and respect Div while they were trapped on Kamino together. He'd been unhappy about the need to keep Div prisoner. Obviously, a part of him considered the mysterious pilot a friend. And it wasn't like Luke to distrust his friends.

"And maybe you're wrong," Luke continued. "But we're never going to know unless we find him."

"That's what we've been *trying* to do," Han reminded him.

"And we've tried everything," Leia told him. "It's time to go back. We need reinforcements."

"Not everything," Luke said, his mouth set in a determined line. "Come on, Artoo."

"Luke, where are you going?" Leia cried as Luke and R2-D2 disappeared into the jungle.

"To find Div!" Luke called back. And then he was gone.

Leia couldn't believe it. She glared at Han.

"What?" he asked.

"Why didn't you stop him?" she said.

"*Me?* Why didn't *you* stop him?"

Leia scowled. "Do I have to do everything?"

"Hey, maybe the kid knows what he's doing," Han said.

"Or maybe he —"

"Shhh!" Han urged her suddenly.

Chewbacca growled softly. "Yeah, buddy, I hear it, too," Han whispered.

A loud rustling came from the jungle. It sounded like it was only a few meters to the west. Han drew his blaster. Leia tightened her grip on her blaster pistol, still in its holster. Without speaking, they positioned themselves back to back so they could cover all sides of the clearing.

The rustling grew louder. Now it was coming from both the east and the west.

"They've got us surrounded," Han whispered. "Stay behind me, Princess. I'll protect you."

"Since when do I need *you* to protect me?" Leia asked irritably. The noise was close now. Close and . . . familiar. "Besides, I don't think —"

"Shhh!" Han hissed. "Just follow my lead and no one will — aaaaaagh!"

A flock of kitehawks erupted out of the trees. They swarmed the clearing. Han started beating them back with his blaster. But that only made them angry. The kitehawks began to emit a high keening noise, and extended their claws. Then, as one, they dive-bombed him. More and more flowed out of the jungle, all heading straight for Han. "Get 'em off me!" Han shouted, nearly vanishing in the dark cloud of kitehawks.

Leia burst into laughter. Kitehawks were harmless. Back on Alderaan, many children kept them as pets. But Han was flailing and shouting as if he were being attacked by a horde of angry clawbirds.

"All right, Chewie," Leia said to the Wookiee, whose hairy shoulders were shaking with laughter. "Should we put him out of his misery?"

In response, Chewbacca threw back his head and let loose an echoing roar. The terrified kitehawks took off as one, vanishing into the trees.

Han's eyes were squeezed shut, his arms waving wildly in an effort to fend off his attackers. It took him a moment to realize they were gone. Finally, he dropped his arms and opened his eyes. "Told you I'd protect you, Your Worshipfulness," he said.

Leia plucked a feather out of his scruffy hair. "Lucky me."

Thorny branches slapped at his face and legs. Luke hacked through them with his lightsaber, forcing his way deeper and deeper into the dense jungle growth. Massassi trees towered overhead, their canopy of leaves blocking out the sun. His feet sank into a soft bed of mud and leaves, and when he passed, it sprang back into place, obliterating his footsteps — as it had obliterated any traces of Div and his captors.

This was pointless. The jungle stretched on for miles in all directions. Luke had picked up a few tracking skills back on Tatooine. But following Jawa tracks across the desert was a lot different from tracking mysterious kidnappers through a jungle. He had no idea where to start.

"What do you think, little guy?" Luke asked R2-D2. The droid beeped at him helplessly.

Luke sighed. "I know. But we *have* to find him."

R2-D2 beeped again, pointing at Luke's lightsaber with his manipulator arm.

"I don't think this is going to help," Luke said, confused. The astromech droid trilled a long series of beeps and whistles, obviously frustrated. Suddenly, Luke understood. "You don't mean that I should use the lightsaber, do you? You mean I should use the *Force!*"

R2-D2 beeped excitedly. His domed head spun in a circle.

Luke shook his head. "I wish I could. I know that's what Ben would have done. But I don't know how."

The astromech droid just pointed to the lightsaber again, insistent.

"I guess I could try," Luke agreed. "What's the worst that could happen?"

He wasn't sure how to start. So he just stood, waiting. Feeling somewhat silly, he closed his eyes and tried to clear his mind of distractions. He focused intently on Div.

Nothing happened.

Come on, Ben, he thought. *Help me out.*

It was so frustrating, knowing he had this power in himself and no way to reach it. If only there was someone to tell him what to do.

Or you could figure it out for yourself.

It wasn't Ben's voice in his head. It was his own.

Luke slowed his breathing. He relaxed his muscles. This time, he didn't try to focus his mind on Div, or on anything. He let his thoughts roam freely, as they did when he was drifting off to sleep. Instead of blocking out the world around him, he soaked it in. The soft mud beneath his boots, the chirps of the chuck-lucks, the rich, heavy scent of the purple Massassi bark. If the jungle had something to tell him, he was listening.

Again, nothing happened. But when Luke opened his eyes, some impulse drove him to look toward the southwest. And he noticed something he hadn't before: a regularity, almost a pattern, in the randomness of the jungle growth. But in one spot it was broken, more branches were bent and more flowers trampled than should have been. Something had come through the trees here. Maybe an animal.

But Luke didn't think so. "Come on, Artoo." He urged the astromech droid to hurry through the trees. "I sure hope this works."

He didn't know if it was the Force that made everything seem sharper, made every twisted branch and shallow footprint jump out in a way they never had before. But he didn't question it. He just followed his instincts. They brought him to a clearing, where a beat-up Firespray ship was powering up its engines. Three men loaded an unconscious figure into the cargo bay. It had to be Div.

Luke was outnumbered and outgunned, with no time to wait for reinforcements. He was going to have to handle this himself.

"Go find the others and tell them I went after Div," Luke said to R2-D2. "Tell them I'll be back."

The droid beeped in alarm, but Luke ignored it. He crept closer to the ship, careful not to let the men see him. Two of the men climbed into the cockpit while the third climbed into the cargo bay. The doors began to slide shut.

It was his best chance. Also his last chance.

Luke ran toward the ship as fast as he could. One man caught sight of him and began to shout, but the noise was drowned out by the thundering engines. As the man fumbled for a blaster, Luke threw himself into the cargo bay. The doors shut behind him as blasterfire sprayed the bulkheads.

"What do you think you're doing?" the man shouted, taking aim at Luke.

Luke activated his lightsaber and struck out blindly. The laserfire bounced off the blue beam and slammed into a large stack of heavy crates. They toppled over, landing squarely on top of the man with the blaster. With a loud *"Oof,"* he collapsed to the floor.

Luke rushed to Div, who lay in a corner, bound and unconscious. "Come on, wake up," he muttered. "We need to get you out of here before —" The engines flared and the ship lifted off the ground. "Before that happens." Luke braced himself against the wall as the ship rocketed through the atmosphere.

It seemed they were going for a ride.

Luke used his lightsaber to cut through Div's restraints. "Div, wake up!" he said again, careful to keep his voice down. But Div didn't move.

Luke was on his own.

He nudged the fallen kidnapper with his foot. The body didn't stir. But there were still two more on the other side of the bulkhead. He'd have to deal with them — preferably *before* they figured out they had a stowaway.

A narrow retractable panel separated the cargo bay from the cockpit. Luke inched it aside and peeked through the slender gap. One of the men bent over the controls, programming something into the autopilot. He ran a hand through his dark red hair, then hesitated over the control panel, as if nervous about the flight path.

"Just do it," growled the other. Tall and muscular, he looked uncomfortable, cramped in the narrow copilot seat. "We got what he wanted. Time for our reward."

"Never heard of him *rewarding* anyone," the redhead muttered.

"First time for everything," the big one said. *"Now."*

There was a rustling behind Luke. He whirled around. Div was stirring. Eyes still closed, Div lashed out with his arm, whacking the plastoid bulkhead.

"Hey, you hear that?" the copilot asked, jumping up from his seat. He opened a channel on the comlink.

Luke held his breath.

"Griff, everything okay with the prisoner?" the copilot asked. "Griff?"

Griff, lying unconscious on the floor of the cargo bay, did not respond.

It was now or never. Luke activated his lightsaber again. Blue blade held high, he burst into the cockpit. The copilot barreled toward him. Luke struck out with the lightsaber, but the man grabbed his arm and twisted hard. Luke swallowed a gasp of pain. He tossed the lightsaber to his other hand. The blade whipped through the air and sliced effortlessly through the man's bulging belly. He dropped to the ground, curled up and cradling the wound.

Laserfire screamed past Luke, scorching the wall behind him.

The pilot stood before the controls, blaster aimed at Luke. "Where did you come from? What do you want?

What'd you do to Tyrus? What's that sword thing? Who *are* you?"

Luke swept his gaze across the tiny cockpit. There was a chance he'd be able to block the laserfire with his lightsaber. But he'd be a lot more confident about blocking it with a chair, or a storage crate, or a nice thick durasteel bulkhead. "Which question do you want me to answer first?" he asked, stalling.

The pilot shrugged. "How about . . . none of them?"

He fired.

Luke ducked, closed his eyes, let the Force guide his hands.

The laserfire smacked into his lightsaber. Luke stumbled backward with the impact.

"Watch it." A voice came from behind him. And then another shot. The pilot clutched his chest and pitched forward, tumbling to the floor. Luke spun around to see Div grinning behind him. "You're welcome," Div said. "Now, what are you doing here?"

"Rescuing you," Luke said.

Div raised an eyebrow. Then he raised his blaster. "Don't move!" he shouted.

Luke froze. But Div wasn't aiming at him.

Groaning with pain, the pilot hoisted himself up to the control panel. "If you want to live, don't move!" Div warned him.

But the pilot didn't stop. He reached toward the controls. Div pulled the trigger. Laserfire sailed across the cockpit, peppering the pilot's body. He tumbled forward onto the controls, his hand slapping down on a large red switch. With a weak but satisfied smile, he dropped to the floor.

And in the viewscreen, the sky exploded with light as the ship jumped into hyperspace.

Stars streamed past as the ship hurtled through space.

Moments later, the autopilot took them out of hyperspace. The ship came to rest in an empty pocket of the galaxy with no planetary systems anywhere in sight. They could have been anywhere. And they had a bigger problem: the Star Destroyer looming in their viewscreen. Hundreds of times their size, the arrow-shaped silver ship hung motionless in the sky less than twenty klicks away, as if it had been waiting for them — which, Div realized, it almost certainly was.

Div glanced at Luke. "When does the rescuing start?" he asked drily.

"Maybe we can escape before it notices us," Luke said, fiddling with the unfamiliar hyperdrive controls.

Div jabbed a boot into the unconscious pilot, hoping the man could give them some clue as to what they were up against. But he didn't stir. Luke was muttering to himself, trying to program a new set of coordinates. "It's an old ship," he murmured. "It's going to take at least six minutes before the drive is ready to jump again."

"I'm not sure we have six minutes," Div said.

The launch hangars of the Star Destroyer slid partially open. A single TIE fighter slipped through the narrow crevice.

"Just one?" Luke said. "We can take it."

"Great," Div said. "But who's going to take *them*?" As he spoke, the hangar doors were sliding wide open. A fleet of TIE fighters poured out, blanketing the sky.

An Imperial transmission came through from the Star Destroyer. "Identify yourselves," a flat, tinny voice commanded. "Imperial authentication and docking codes required."

Luke took a weapons inventory while Div again tried to rouse the pilot, shaking him and propping him on his feet. No luck.

"A few concussion missiles and a defective laser cannon," Luke said quickly. "That's it."

Enough to dispatch three, maybe four TIE fighters. No more.

"Identify yourselves," the voice said again.

Div lunged for the comm. "We're here on official Imperial business," he said quickly. "We're expected."

The voice was unimpressed. "Identification and authorization. Now."

"How long before the hyperdrive is ready?" Div said.

"Four minutes now."

"Okay, we definitely don't have four minutes," Div said. He powered up the missile launchers. It wasn't much, but it would have to do.

The comm buzzed with an incoming message. But this wasn't coming from the Star Destroyer. It was coming from one of the TIE fighters.

"That's a Rebel frequency!" Luke exclaimed. They bent their heads together over the transmission, eyes widening in surprise. The TIE fighter had sent them a set of Imperial docking codes.

That wasn't all the TIE fighter had sent them. The message also included coordinates to be input into the hyperdrive. The TIE fighter was sending them somewhere. It was the strangest rescue Div had ever seen.

Or it was a trap.

F O U R

A kind face leans over him, and blond hair brushes his forehead. Her lips skim his cheek, and she smiles. She smells like zinthorn blossoms. Sleep now, she says in her soft, musical voice. He feels safe. He feels at home.

X-7 jerked the speeder back in its lane, a split second before ramming into a blue airspeeder.

"Watch it, you kreetle!" shouted the Trandoshan at the wheel, shaking a clawed fist at X-7's jet-black speeder.

"Focus," X-7 murmured, weaving through the dense Coruscant traffic. One trillion people swarmed the surface of this planet-sized city, and at the moment, it seemed all of them were crowding the skylanes of Quadrant 472. Trast speeder trucks and Zzip Astral-8s and SoroSuubs of every shape and color jockeyed for position as they whizzed past the skyscrapers, burrowing into the city like gravel-maggots infesting a rotting muja fruit. X-7 didn't possess the normal human inclination to prefer one environment over another. The mountains of Julio, the plains of Loped VII, the breathtaking cliffs of Kenosha, the bare, craggy surface of a lifeless moon — they were all the same to him. But if he *had* had a preference, this would be its opposite. The crystalline spires glowing in the blazing red sunset, the millions of windows glinting in the dying light, the layers upon layers of *people* covering every inch of the surface, buildings stretching untold kilometers into the sky — it was supposed to be the pride of the galaxy. It gave X-7 a headache.

Navigating the skylanes demanded his full attention. But how was he supposed to concentrate with these wretched *memories* floating around in his head?

"I dare you!" the boy cries.

"No, I dare you!" he shouts back.

The boy laughs and steers his speeder bike straight for the edge of the ravine. He surges forward at top speed, then pulls up at the very last minute. The momentum carries him across. He waves from the other side. "Your turn now, you sprigging coward!"

He is afraid. But he is also determined. He leans forward. Pushes the throttle. Wind thunders in his ears. The ground opens beneath him, and he is flying —

"Enough!" X-7 shouted. Blind with rage, he rammed the speeder into the bright red sport speeder in front of him, knocking the sport into a wild spin across four levels of traffic. The sport crashed into a zip speeder, which smashed into two Flash speeders. Crushed and twisted durasteel spiraled through the air; drivers moaned and cried; sirens screamed. And X-7 quietly steered his heavily armored Serous into a narrow alleyway, fleeing the chaos he'd caused.

The needless destruction made him feel better. And that was the problem.

Feeling angry.

Feeling better.

Feeling anything at all. It wasn't right. He wasn't built for it. He was a *tool,* not a person. How many times had his commander burned that message into his brain? The Commander, who had taken X-7's flesh-and-blood form and molded it into something better, something *perfect.* Scooped out his mind, purging it of memories, of emotions, of *weakness,* and turning his will to durasteel.

All these years, X-7 would have *felt* grateful, if he could have felt anything at all.

But now everything was going wrong. It had started with the *feelings.* Frustration, impatience, rage. They'd clouded his mind; that was why he hadn't been able to complete his mission, he told himself. It was why Skywalker still lived. And the more often Skywalker foiled him, the angrier he grew.

Then, as if the feelings had wedged open a long-sealed vault, the memories had arrived. Not even memories — just flashes, really. Nothing he could grab hold of or understand. A too-familiar scent. A few notes of a long-forgotten song. A voice. And now, it was even worse, these incomplete moments, confusing stories from someone else's life. As nonsensical as a dream.

Dreaming. Something else X-7 wasn't supposed to be capable of.

He was broken.

He must be broken, because that was the only possible explanation for his not wanting to be fixed. For his suddenly having *wants,* which were as alien as the *feelings.* For his disobeying a direct order from his commander to return for retraining.

It was why instead he was here, guiding his speeder into the alley behind the Commander's building, with an armory of weapons on the seat beside him.

He didn't *want* retraining. He *wanted* answers.

The thirty-story building was home to several third-rate Imperial officers, those deemed unworthy of space in the more desirable Imperial headquarters. On the plus side, being this far from the Emperor meant less chance of running into Lord Vader in the hallway. On the other hand, placement in this quadrant was often the first stop to a far less appealing posting: the Outer Rim perhaps. Or to being "promoted" to commandant on a prison moon, forced to live out the rest of one's life eating diluted gruel, administering executions, and waiting to die.

X-7's research had revealed that this was likely to be

his master's fate—although the Commander himself hadn't yet figured that out.

The building was stocked with a full complement of stormtroopers in addition to the handful of Imperial has-beens and never-weres. But again, they were hardly the cream of the crop. With a little stealth and some cheap false docs, X-7 could have waltzed into the Commander's office without notice.

He chose not to.

The docs brought him into the building and onto the turbolift. But when he reached the sixty-second floor, he stepped out with his dart shooter in hand. It was small enough to be concealed in his palm; the guards never knew what was coming. He aimed for the small pocket of flesh just below their helmets and above their body armor—a little-known but fatal weakness. One stormtrooper, two, three, toppled to the floor with a sat-isfying clatter. Three more dropped, leaving only one on his feet. On a whim, X-7 decided to give him a chance to fire. Lasers shot from the blaster, peppering the wall of the turbolift as X-7 dodged the beams. The stormtrooper charged, and X-7 leapt out of the way, firing a blaster as he soared through the air.

The stormtrooper screamed and dropped to the floor beside his friends.

X-7 had hoped a little exercise might leave him calmer for his encounter with the Commander. Killing was always a good pressure release. But not this time.

No matter, X-7 thought. *I'll have likely more to do on the way out.*

He blasted the lock on the Commander's office door. Soresh leapt out of his chair, reaching for a switch above his desk. "What the —"

X-7 streaked across the room and slapped a hand over the Commander's mouth. He pressed a blaster to the Commander's temple. "Your security team has been taken care of," he informed the Commander. "All the same, I'd prefer you not to press your silent alarm. Please."

Very slowly, the Commander lowered his arm.

"Sit down," X-7 ordered him.

It was strange giving orders to his master: No satisfaction in it. But he had no intention of hurting the Commander. He just wanted answers. And he'd run out of options.

"When I invited you to return home, X-7, this isn't quite what I meant," the Commander said lightly.

"I want to know who I am," X-7 said. He stayed behind his master, partly because it was the strategically stronger position, but mostly because it was easier not having to see his face.

"You are X-7, agent to the Emperor," the Commander said. "The Empire's most skillful assassin . . . until recently, that is."

As always, the reminder of his failure pained him. "Who I *was*," X-7 said gruffly. "Before *this*."

The Commander shook his head. "You're smarter than that. Whoever that person was, he's dead. Your brain is no longer equipped for human emotions, human memories. Trying to dredge them up again would probably drive you to madness." He paused. "Perhaps it's already begun? If that's what's going on here, X-7, if you're starting to *feel* things, I can help you —"

"No!" Only the truth would help him. Finding out who he was, the whole story, was the only way to decipher the flashes — and make them go away. If he could find that person he'd once been, he could purge all traces of him, once and for all. He could be pure. The Commander couldn't do that for him. X-7 needed to do it for himself.

Wanted to do it.

That was the only reason for this, he told himself. It wasn't some foolish effort to regain his past. It was a *mission*, the only way he could heal himself and continue to serve his commander. That was all that mattered, *feelings* or not.

"You're determined?" the Commander asked. "Nothing I say can convince you this is a disastrous idea?"

"Nothing," X-7 confirmed.

The Commander sighed. "I can't tell you who you were, because even I don't know," he said. "But I can tell you how to find out."

X-7 felt his lips curling upward; he felt something warm radiate across his chest.

It was repulsive, humiliating, but inescapable: He felt happy.

Footsteps pounded down the hallway, approaching the office. Reinforcements were on their way. Quickly, the Commander gave him a series of passwords that would let him dig deep into the bowels of the Imperial computer system. X-7 took the information, along with several files pertaining to Project Omega's methods for selecting and training its candidates. Then, without a word to the Commander, he ran full speed at the huge window overlooking the city. A shower of transparisteel exploded as he dropped into the sky.

Soresh peered out the window. No bloody figure lay sprawled on the ground sixty-two stories below. Not that he could see clearly through the layers of clogged skylanes. But Soresh was almost certain that X-7 wasn't down there. He'd have had liquid cable, or grappling hooks, or an airspeeder on autopilot waiting beneath the window, *some* kind of backup plan. He was too smart not to. Soresh should know: X-7 was his creation.

The stormtroopers blasted through the door, their weapons drawn. "Sir! Sir! Is everything all right in here?"

Soresh rolled his eyes. The incompetence was breathtaking. He made a mental note to take down all their ID numbers. They'd be dodging energy spiders in the Spice Mines of Kessel by the end of the week. "It is *now*," he snapped. "What took you so long?"

"It was a sneak attack, sir," the lead stormtrooper said. "They took down your entire security detail."

"They?" Soresh arched an eyebrow. "I think you mean '*he*.' One man took down seven of your most finely trained men?" At least he wouldn't have to go to the trouble of punishing them for their failures. That was one bright note to the dark day. And perhaps their replacements would be *competent*. Although he doubted it. The Empire was having a harder and harder time finding good people — just one of the reasons that Soresh had such high hopes for Project Omega. When men's minds were properly molded, there was no place for incompetence, no room for error. When you built a man from the ground up, he became incapable of disobedience or failure.

Or at least, that was the way it was supposed to work.

"Dismissed," he told the stormtroopers, waving them out of the office. Pathetic.

Of course things would have been easier if the stormtroopers had done their job and taken X-7 into custody. But Soresh hadn't been afraid. X-7 would not have hurt him. It was the prime directive of his programming: His commander's life was supreme. Soresh could only imagine how much pain defying his orders must be causing X-7. Attempting to *injure* his master? The pain would have been unbearable.

And perhaps it was better this way. The information Soresh had provided would send X-7 on a fruitless chase across the galaxy. He would find no answers to his questions; no answers could be found. All participants in Project Omega had their former identities completely wiped from the system, and had their faces surgically altered to ensure no awkward encounters with people from their past. X-7 was chasing a ghost. And when he realized that, he would eventually return to the fold, to his commander, to Soresh. He would be repaired. And if that didn't work, he would be terminated.

It was hardly the most pressing of problems.

Soresh's comlink buzzed. He drew in a sharp breath. It was an incoming transmission from Lord Vader.

Now he was afraid. Soresh told himself that Darth Vader couldn't have heard about X-7's misbehavior. But if he had — if word had leaked out — it could put the future of Project Omega in jeopardy. And if Vader was taking a personal interest for some reason . . . well, everyone knew what happened to those who found themselves on Vader's bad side. And it seemed all he had were bad sides.

Soresh gathered his nerve. It galled him that Vader could do this to him, make him cower and tremble.

But then, he was a cowardly man. He'd always known this about himself, detested it until he recognized it for what it was: a sign of his intelligence. Cowards were simply people who knew how to survive. It was the fools with no fear who died prematurely.

Vader's time was coming.

Soresh promised himself that. Then he took the call.

"Yes, Lord Vader?" he said in as even a voice as he could muster.

For several long moments, there was nothing but the sound of Vader's labored breathing. When he finally spoke, his voice filled the room. The lights even seemed to dim in deference to Lord Vader's dark presence.

"I am displeased," Vader said.

Soresh shuddered, imagining the *thing* behind that black mask focusing its rage on him. Everyone knew that it was unwise to speculate on what kind of monster lay beneath Vader's elaborate armor. But everyone had their suspicions.

Their nightmares.

"Lord Vader, I assure you, it's just a momentary malfunction, nothing to trouble yourself about, and certainly Project Omega can continue as —"

"Silence!" Vader said. "Your pointless project means nothing to me."

Soresh knew enough not to speak.

"The Rebel pilot," Vader said, an ominous note of

warning in his voice. "The one responsible for blowing up the Death Star. You are to stop your pursuit of him."

No one knew of his secret plan to hunt down Luke Skywalker. No one but X-7, and malfunction or not, he'd never go crying to Vader. "What makes you think—"

"Consider your next words very *carefully*," Vader advised.

Soresh had heard rumors of Vader's power. It was said he could suffocate a man with a thought, from across the room. It was said that his powers extended across the reach of space, that he could strike a man down wherever he stood. Of course, they were just rumors.

Probably.

"The Emperor has made it a top priority to hunt down that pilot," Soresh said. He was determined to prove himself to the Emperor and gain the respect he deserved. But he wasn't intending to do it by going head to head with Vader. He'd watched his colleagues make that stupid mistake again and again. None of them had survived the attempt. "As a loyal servant of the Empire, I of course hope to do whatever I can to further the Emperor's goals."

Beneath the words lay his real meaning: *I serve the Emperor, not you.*

"The Emperor cannot be troubled to concern himself with the fate of a single Rebel pilot — or a single Imperial commander," Vader replied.

The meaning behind his words was equally clear: *The Emperor won't protect you, not from me.*

"Return your attention to your own affairs," Vader said. "Leave Skywalker to *me.*"

The transmission cut off abruptly. Soresh opened his desk drawer and pulled out his flask of Dorian Quill. He took a long swig.

His hands were shaking.

But amid the terror, his mind was spinning. Vader knew the pilot's name — perhaps had known all along? And yet instead of hunting him down, as the Emperor desired, Vader was letting the man live free. At least for now. And he was warning Soresh to stay away. Because he wanted the glory of the kill all to himself?

Maybe, Soresh thought.

But maybe it was something else. Something Vader didn't want anyone to know about.

Something that could destroy him.

CHAPTER FIVE

The digits flashed on the screen, waiting for Luke to make a decision. Or rather, a series of decisions, each of which could get them killed.

Input the Imperial docking codes — and, if the codes were false, risk being blown to bits by a fleet of TIE fighters. Or ignore the Imperial docking codes — and risk being blown to bits by a fleet of TIE fighters.

Even if he did transmit the docking codes and they worked, then what? Attempt to board the Star Destroyer and find out exactly what the Empire wanted from Lune Divinian? Buy themselves enough time to follow their mysterious helper's instructions and take a hyperspace jump to who-knew-where? Or flee back to Yavin 4, without answers — but with their lives?

"I think we should go for it," Div said suddenly. "I . . . I just have a good feeling about this."

"You want to make a decision based on a *hunch*?"

Luke asked, knowing exactly what Han would have to say about that. And yet Div had put his finger on exactly what Luke was feeling. Was that the Force, telling him that the mysterious TIE fighter was trustworthy?

Or was it just wishful thinking?

Aware that time was running out, Luke closed his eyes, trying to connect with his instincts. But when he did, all he saw was X-7's sneering face — a cold reminder of what happened when you trusted the wrong person. There were always consequences.

"Trust your instincts," Div said, and at the sound of his voice, the image of X-7 fell away. "And in the meantime, get ready to fire."

Trust your feelings, echoed a voice in his head. Ben's voice.

His feelings were telling him that an ally was nearby. A friend. But was that friend in the TIE fighter, helping him escape — or was the friend a prisoner desperate to be rescued from the Star Destroyer? What if the TIE fighter was just trying to send Luke on a wild-goose chase so he wouldn't discover the truth?

The seconds were ticking by, and the TIE fighters were powering up their weapons. But Luke had learned something else from Ben: Hasty action could often be more dangerous than inaction. Sometimes it was best to wait until you were sure.

"Luke, make a drokking decision or —"

A spurt of laserfire burst out of the nearest TIE fighter and slammed into the ship, which bucked beneath them. Luke was thrown off his feet. He flew backward, slamming into the rear bulkhead. A sharp pain radiated through his head and down his spine. Div was saying something, but Luke couldn't take it in. His ears were ringing. Red spots swam across his field of vision. The ship shuddered as Div fired toward the TIE fighters. Smoke billowed from the sensor array. Luke shook his head, trying to clear it. Unsteady but determined, he pulled himself to his feet.

Div was frantically trying to keep them alive. But they were wildly outnumbered, and they'd already used most of their missiles. As for evasive maneuvers, the ship handled about as well as a three-legged dewback.

They were a sitting target.

Laserfire lit up the sky as TIE fighters swarmed. Then, without warning, one of the fighters turned on its own. Its laser cannons fired a blast at the nearest Imperial ship. The ship shattered, sending debris spinning wildly into the rest of the fleet. The renegade TIE fighter was everywhere at once, picking its way through the Imperial fleet, taking them down one by one.

It was all the distraction Luke needed.

He activated the hyperdrive, hoping they wouldn't end up inside a sun.

They jumped.

• • •

Light streamed past the viewscreen as they blazed through hyperspace. Smears of stars streaked across the black of space. And then, after an instant that felt like an eternity, the stars were stars again, points of light in the darkness. Space was silent, still, and empty. They had arrived.

Somewhere.

"I hope you're right about this," Luke said nervously.

"Me? You're the one who powered up the hyperdrive and took a blind jump."

"You'd rather we sat waiting to be blown out of the sky?" Luke argued, annoyed. He *knew* that Div would have done the same thing if he'd had the chance. He was obviously just irritated that Luke had moved faster. "Besides, you're the one who said we could trust this guy."

"I don't trust anyone," Div said.

As he spoke, a TIE fighter appeared out of hyperspace.

"That's impossible!" Luke exclaimed. "TIE fighters don't have hyperdrives!"

"Feel free to complain to the Empire," Div said, manning the missile launchers. "*I'm* going to get the weapons ready. You know, just in case the impossible TIE fighter decides to blow us out of the sky."

It seemed likely the TIE fighter was the same ship that had sent them the coordinates, though there was no way to tell. But now it was battle-scarred, deep gashes running up and down its hull. It had clearly taken some heavy fire before jumping, which meant the pilot, whoever he was, must have been good. TIE fighters weren't built to withstand much fire. Imperial pilots, like their ships, were considered infinitely replaceable.

Of course, the ships also weren't built to make hyperspace jumps. Obviously this was no ordinary TIE fighter—which meant it was likely no ordinary pilot.

Ignoring them, the ship maneuvered into orbit around a nearby moon and disappeared into the thin atmosphere. A transmission came through, on the same Rebel frequency used before. More coordinates, this time for a landing spot on the face of the moon.

Luke and Div exchanged a glance.

"We've come this far," Luke said, and took the Firespray down to the surface.

The atmosphere was thick enough that they could breathe but thin enough that they could still see the stars. The moon was dead, arid, flat, and small. In the distance, Luke could make out the curve of the horizon. They stayed in the ship, keeping their weapons trained on the TIE fighter. Its hatch opened, and a figure stepped out. He was dressed in the uniform of an Imperial pilot, but an Imperial pilot would never be so out of shape. As the man drew closer to the ship, Luke glimpsed his face. He nearly laughed in relief. "Come on," he told Div. "It's okay. He's a friend." He flung open the hatch of the

Firespray and hurried to meet their rescuer, a man he'd never expected to see again. Ferus Olin.

Div followed slowly.

"Luke," Ferus said when Luke had reached him. He didn't seem at all surprised.

"Ferus, I can't believe it!" Luke said. He'd met Ferus Olin on Delaya, the sister planet to Alderaan. The old man had known Leia when she was a child, and he'd quickly proven himself to be a brave and solid ally. Luke had hoped he would join the Rebel Alliance, but he had refused. *He has a mission of his own,* Leia had said, sounding skeptical. *Or he's just too cowardly to fight.* But Ferus hadn't seemed like a coward, not to Luke. He'd seemed wise and oddly trustworthy. His very presence was comforting, as if he always knew more than what he was saying, and was ready to face it. *Just like Ben,* Luke thought, not for the first time.

Ferus was the last person he would have expected to meet on this strange moon, especially piloting a TIE fighter and dressed in Imperial uniform. But there was almost no one else he would rather have seen.

"Div, this is Ferus—" Luke broke off as he spotted Div's ashen face. He was standing stiffly, like a soldier at attention. His hand twitched toward his holster, as if he was fighting the temptation to draw. "It's okay," Luke assured him. "Ferus is a friend."

"I'm pretty sure you don't know *who* this is," Div said

quietly, glaring at Ferus. The older man's eyes widened.

Luke looked back and forth between them, confused. "Do you two know each other?"

Before anyone could answer, Ferus swept him into a fierce bear hug. "I've been worried about you, Luke. Glad to see you're all right."

The hug seemed somewhat strange; he didn't know Ferus *that* well. But he didn't want to be rude. "No need to worry," he told Ferus. "I'm fine."

Something pricked the back of his neck. He slapped at it. Probably a banda bug, he thought idly. Although this moon looked pretty dead. Not a likely environment for a banda — no food for them to nibble on.

And why was he thinking about bandas?

Why were his thoughts flying in a million directions, like a flock of frightened hawk-bats?

Why did he suddenly feel like the ground was buckling beneath him?

Luke opened his mouth but lacked the strength to speak. In fact, he realized, he lacked the strength to do much of anything.

And then he was on the ground, staring up at the night sky.

I'm so tired, he thought. *Why am I so tired?*

But he was too tired to wonder for very long.

Instead, he closed his eyes.

And went to sleep.

CHAPTER SIX

"**L**uke needs us!" Leia shouted. Why wouldn't anyone on Yavin 4 understand?

"I fear that may be, Your Highness," General Rieekan said, "but we have no way of knowing where he is. I can't authorize a fool's mission."

"Are you calling me a *fool*, General?" Leia asked coolly.

Han cleared his throat. "I'm sure the general's not —"

"The general can speak for himself," Leia snapped.

General Rieekan sighed and shook his head. "The answer is no, Your Highness. I'm sorry."

Leia turned her back on both of them and stormed out of the temple. She heard Han behind her and picked up her pace. As he walked faster, she began to run. He didn't catch up with her until they'd nearly arrived at the hangar deck.

"Where do you think you're going?" Han asked, grabbing her as she headed toward the nearest and fastest craft. She shrugged him off.

"Isn't it obvious? I'm going to find Luke!"

"And how, exactly, are you going to do that, Your Worshipfulness? You gonna fly around in circles with your eyes closed and just wait to run into him?"

"I have to do *something,* Han! Are you coming or not?"

"This is crazy, Leia. You heard General Rieekan —"

"You're siding with *him*?" Leia couldn't believe it. Han had never turned down the opportunity to do something crazy. *Never.* But now that Luke's life was at stake, *now* he wanted to talk about doing the sensible thing? Leia was angry; felt helpless. *Of course* she knew that a rescue mission was foolish. Of course she knew logically that there was almost no chance of her finding Luke. The galaxy was a big place, and she didn't even know where to start. But . . . it was *Luke.* She was convinced that something would guide her to him. It always did. "Don't you see, Han?" she cried, frustrated. "I have to."

"Have to what, Princess? Spend the rest of your life jumping to random coordinates, shouting his name out the window? You really think that's going to work?"

"At least I'm doing something," she retorted. "Unlike *you.* You're happy just sitting around doing *nothing.*"

Han grimaced at her. "Listen, lady, if you think this

makes me happy—" He stopped himself, then murmured something under his breath. Leia suddenly realized he was counting to ten. When he spoke again, his voice was even. "The kid'll be fine. He's gotten himself out of plenty of tight spaces. Tighter than this."

"You don't even know what 'this' is."

"Yeah, but I know Luke. The kid's not about to go down without a fight."

"Exactly. Which is why some of us are trying to fight for him."

"Some of us?" So much for counting to ten. Han's anger was back. "Guess I don't have to ask who 'some of us' is. So I don't care? That's what you're saying?"

"Look at you, Han! You have less feeling than a droid!" She nodded toward the *Millennium Falcon,* where C-3PO was becoming hysterical. R2-D2 beeped soothingly.

"What do you mean, 'this always happens, and he always survives'?" C-3PO asked indignantly. "Nothing like this has ever—"

R2-D2 beeped again.

"Oh. Yes," C-3PO said. "But that was different, because on Kamino he—"

The astromech trilled, his lights flashing.

"That was different, *too,*" C-3PO insisted. "Who knew he could survive a Podracer explosion? But this, *this* . . . Oh dear, Artoo, I just don't know what I'll do if something happens to Master Luke. This is a catastrophe!"

Han snorted. "Look, Princess, you don't get this yet, but maybe someday when you're a little older, a little more experienced —"

"*Excuse* me?" In principle, Leia believed that physical violence should be used only when all other courses of action had been exhausted. In practice, she was about ready to punch him in the gut.

"— you'll see that someone has to stay calm. Be strong. You can't just run around panicking about every little thing that goes wrong. You should take things like a —" He spotted Chewbacca emerging from the *Millennium Falcon*. "Well, like a Wookiee." He slapped Chewbacca on his furry back. "Right, pal? Go on, tell her Luke's going to be just fine."

At Luke's name, Chewbacca threw back his giant head and unleashed a mournful roar.

Han looked at Chewie in disgust.

"I don't care what you say," Leia said fiercely, starting toward the ship again. "I don't care what anyone says. I'm going to find Luke."

"Leia!" Han grabbed her arm and, this time, refused to let go. "We have to trust him," he said, the mocking tone gone from his voice. "That's the best thing we can do right now. It's all we can do. We've got to trust him to come back to us."

"But . . ." She didn't want to admit he was right. She *couldn't* just sit here and wait. It was too frustrating.

Too terrifying.

"He'll be okay," Han said, still gripping her arm. "He'll be back."

"You really believe that?" Leia peered intently into his eyes. Han was an excellent liar, but he'd never been very good at lying to her.

"I really do," he said. But as he answered, he looked away.

"Please don't," Ferus said mildly as Div snatched the lightsaber from Luke's belt. Ignoring the older man, Div activated the Jedi weapon. Ferus kept his eyes fixed on the gleaming blue beam. Div kept his eyes fixed on Ferus.

Ferus Olin, after all these years. A fairy-tale hero from his childhood. Ferus, who'd had all the answers.

Ferus, who'd turned his back and walked away.

May the Force be with you, Lune, he had said as Ferus prepared to leave. At the time, Lune was dimly aware that his mother had fallen in love with Clive Flax and that together they would be starting a new life and a new family. But all he really cared about was that he was getting a new brother. Trever, the teenaged orphan from Bellassa who needed a home. *Take care of Trever,* Ferus told Lune. Trever was like a son to Ferus — yet here he was, leaving the boy behind.

Ferus had said one more thing before saying good-bye forever: *You would have made a fine Jedi.*

With Garen Muln and Ry-Gaul dead, Ferus was the only person left in the galaxy who could teach Lune the Jedi way. And Ferus was saying good-bye. At the time, Lune had just grinned, thinking that it was a compliment. Not realizing everything he was about to lose.

Ferus hadn't aged well. The lithe, resolute man Div remembered, the proud Jedi with laugh lines creasing his worried face and a defiant gaze that dared the world to cross him, that person was gone. In his place was a prematurely old man with gray hair and a soft, bulging belly. As far as Div could tell, everything about him was soft. Since the last time they'd met, nearly twenty years before, Div had become a warrior. And Ferus had apparently become a Corellian cream puff. Though that cream puff had just put Luke on the ground.

Div would never have imagined that Ferus Olin, of all people, would turn to the dark side. But there he was, flying a TIE fighter. There he was, standing over Luke's unconscious form.

People changed.

"You've grown," Ferus said, a smile creeping across his face. He seemed unconcerned by the lightsaber aimed at his throat.

He still has the Force, Div reminded himself. The man might have grown old and soft, but he could likely disarm Div with a single thought.

"It's good to see you again, Lune," Ferus said softly. "Better than I could have imagined."

"Don't call me that. It's Div."

Lune was a child, who had needed protecting. A prodigy, a Force-sensitive. A hope. Lune was *special*, according to those who had died for him. Lune was the naive child who'd been stuffed into an escape pod, blasted off from the asteroid, leaving his friends behind, stranded. Brave Rebels before the Rebellion, they sent their one and only hope flying to safety, then waited to die. Lune was the boy who'd floated through space in an escape pod, helpless, *useless,* as an energy bolt slammed into the asteroid and blasted it into debris. And then, years later, when the scars had finally healed, Lune had sat on a hilltop and watched his entire family die.

Div was a man. He had only one thing in common with that ignorant boy: He was a survivor.

"I take it this is as much of a joyous reunion as I can expect?" Ferus said with a glimmer of his familiar dry wit.

"Is he going to be all right?" Div asked, glancing at Luke.

Ferus nodded. "Sleep dart. He'll be awake in an hour or so. I needed to buy us some time to talk — privately. There are certain things about me that Luke doesn't need to know."

"Like the fact that you're a Jedi," Div guessed.

"And does your friend know that *you* are?" Ferus asked.

"He's no friend. And I'm no Jedi."

Ferus didn't reply. He just looked pointedly at the lightsaber in Div's hand. As always, it felt so right. Like a piece of him too long absent had finally returned. Div deactivated the weapon and returned it to Luke's side. He had turned away from that life and away from the Force. He had lived with that empty hole inside him, that knowledge that he could have been something more, for a long time. The pain was no longer raw. It was tolerable.

Div scowled at Ferus. "Fine. The kid's out of the way. So here we are. You want to talk? Talk."

"Help me carry him?" Ferus said, kneeling before Luke's body. It was beyond lucky that he'd been able to sense Luke's presence in the Firespray. The Force was strong in Luke, very strong. "It's not safe out here in the open." Together, they lifted the unconscious Rebel and carried him toward the small shelter Ferus had been using as his base. They worked in silence. Ferus kept his head down but spread his attention, absorbing every detail of Lune with his peripheral vision. He had a feeling the boy wouldn't take kindly to being stared at. But it was tempting to do so.

It hurt seeing himself reflected in Lune's expression.

The boy had once looked at him with respect, trusting, with the innocence of a child — the *ignorance* of a child — that Ferus would protect him. More than once, that trust, that duty to protect Lune, had been the only tether keeping Ferus from a bottomless fall into the dark side of the Force. But now . . . Ferus could feel Lune's disgust, his dismay at seeing what his old friend had become. How soft and flabby Ferus had grown over the years. How old.

How cowardly.

Lune couldn't be expected to see beneath Ferus's disguise, to understand that he'd spent decades hiding in plain sight, pretending to be a harmless, senseless courtier. And Ferus couldn't explain it to him, not without explaining *why* it had been so imperative to disguise himself. Not without revealing the secret of Leia Organa, the child Ferus had been sworn to protect. Anakin's child.

Leia was the second child Ferus had sworn to protect, the second "galactic hope." Lune had been the first.

He's alive, Ferus told himself. That was something.

But it wasn't everything.

Ferus had long ago accepted that his mission would mean losing the respect of all around him, even Leia herself. Only Obi-Wan understood who Ferus truly was, and Obi-Wan was dead. This, too, Ferus had finally accepted. Much as he might have craved it, he didn't need Lune's admiration. So what hurt the most wasn't the look on Lune's face; it was the look in his eyes.

As Ferus had grown soft, Lune had grown hard. The boy Ferus remembered — sweet-tempered, mischievous, preternaturally smart, hopeful — that boy was gone. The man who appeared in his place shared many of his qualities, especially that quiet, intensely watchful mode that had seemed eerie in a young boy. But this man was cold and rigid, as if a layer of thick, tough scar tissue had crusted over his soul.

Suddenly, Lune looked up and met his eyes. "Take a holopic," he suggested caustically. "It'll last longer."

Something else the man had in common with the boy, Ferus observed: He still saw more than anyone expected.

"It's been too long," Ferus said softly. "I've thought of you often over the years. You and —"

"How do you know Luke?" Lune asked sharply. "What are you doing here on this cursed moon? What are *we* doing here?"

He doesn't want me to say Trever's name, Ferus thought. *Because he can't stand to hear it? Or he can't stand to hear it from me?*

"Fair enough," he said aloud. "I was an acquaintance of Princess Leia Organa on Alderaan. After the . . . disaster, I found the princess again, and came to know several of her friends. Good people."

"Apparently not good enough for you to tell them the truth about who you really are."

"If you'll let me explain, I think you'll see why it's important Luke not know I'm a Jedi," Ferus said, stalling for time. What was he supposed to say: *I'm keeping the secret because the ghost of a dead Jedi Master warned me that Luke wasn't ready*?

"Oh, I see," Lune spat out. "If the Empire knew the truth, you'd be a target. And if the Rebels knew the truth, they might expect you to *do* something. But you've become a coward. So you stay hidden."

"You think that little of me?" Ferus asked.

"I don't think of you at all," Lune said. "Not since I was a child, and you abandoned us all to die."

"I never abandoned you," Ferus said. "You had your mother and Clive, and—"

"And *I* was supposed to protect him, isn't that right?" Lune said sourly. "That's what you told me, before you left, that I should *take care of Trever*. I was a child. A *child*! You were a *Jedi*, and who were you protecting? Only yourself."

Ferus shook his head. "I thought you would be safe," he said desperately. "All of you. I had a mission—"

"So did they, that day," Lune said bitterly. "They all had missions. My mother. My father. *Trever*."

Ferus flinched at the name.

"You think you know what happened to them," Lune said. "I can see it on your face."

"And I'm so sorry for your loss," Ferus began.

"But you can't know. Not unless you were there. Like *I* was. But I was only fifteen, and they wouldn't let me go with them. Even though I could have helped. So I watched them from a hill overlooking the factory. Like lizard-ants, swarming across the grounds, shooting, running, dying."

Ferus wanted to stop listening. As Lune went on, relating their deaths in horrifying detail, Ferus wanted to summon the Force around his ears like a thick blanket, drowning out the noise. But he made himself hear it all. A Rebel mission betrayed from the inside. An ambush. His old friend Clive cut down where he stood, ripped through by blasterfire. Lune's mother, Astri, fierce and proud, blown to bits by an Imperial grenade. And Trever. Trever, who had survived as an orphan on the streets of Bellassa when he was only a teenager, until Ferus had turned him into a soldier and a fugitive. Trever, who had died a prisoner, trapped inside the munitions factory when the concussion missiles rained down and the building imploded.

"Enough!" Ferus finally cried. He laid Luke's body out on a narrow cot, then lowered himself to the edge, resting a hand on the boy's shoulder. Only then did he notice that his hand was trembling. "Please, Lune," he said quietly. "Enough."

"It's Div."

And Ferus nodded, acknowledging that it was true. "I'm sorry for what happened to them," he said. "And for what's happened to you."

"Nothing happened to me."

Ferus sighed.

"Don't," Div said harshly. "Don't you dare judge *me*. So I'm different from the kid you remember? Look at *you*. Those people we used to be? They're gone. Erased. Whatever it takes to survive, right? That's what makes you and me special. Not the lightsaber, not the Force. We're survivors. Whatever it takes."

The words were proud, but the tone was ashamed. Ferus lowered his head. Lune was just trying to wound him, Ferus knew. He was lashing out, angry about the past, angry about having a reminder of all the things he'd worked hard to forget. Angry that Ferus had left in the first place, then had had the temerity to come back. They were just words.

But shame flooded him nonetheless. The truth hurt.

Luke opened his eyes. The world was blurry. "What happened?" Gradually, the blurs of color before him resolved themselves into faces. Ferus and Div peered down at him, wearing curiously similar expressions.

"You passed out," Div said, then hesitated. He locked eyes with Ferus, and for several moments, a heavy silence settled between them. "You must have hit your head harder than you thought," Div said. "In the ship."

Luke rubbed the spot where his head had slammed into the bulkhead. He felt a small lump, painful to the touch. Still, something seemed off. "My head doesn't hurt that much," he said dubiously.

"Head injuries can be tricky," Ferus said quickly, helping him off the cot. "All the more reason to return to the Rebel Base. And quickly. We have work to do."

"Work? What do you mean?"

Ferus and Div exchanged another of those mysterious glances. Luke wondered how long he'd been out and what had happened between the two of them. It was as if they'd known each other for years rather than minutes.

"That ship you commandeered was on a rendezvous course with an Imperial Star Destroyer," Ferus explained.

"I noticed," Luke said, rubbing the lump on his head again. If they hadn't escaped in time . . . Speaking of which . . . "What were you doing in a TIE fighter?" Luke asked suddenly. "And how'd you find us? And—"

"It's a long story," Ferus said. "And I can tell you on the way. Right now all you need to know is that the pilot of that ship—the one who kidnapped you, Div—was an agent of Darth Vader. The information he gathered is crucial to the Rebel cause. To you in particular, Luke. It's the key to saving your life . . . and, if we're lucky, to ending Vader's."

CHAPTER SEVEN

I t had been foolish to hope that Leia would be happy to see him. Ferus knew that.

But he'd hoped anyway.

Was it his destiny to seemingly disappoint everyone he cared about?

It was so good to see Lune again — *Div*, he reminded himself. And to see him with Luke and Leia, as if the Force itself was drawing them together, readying them for the fight to come.

But it was also unsettling. Years before, Ferus had worked hard to bring Jedi and Force-sensitives together, to draw them out of hiding, prepare them for battle. Obi-Wan had warned him against it, had said it was too soon. (Just as he now said, from beyond the grave, that it was too soon to alert Luke and Leia to their destiny.) But Ferus had gone forward anyway — and they had all died.

Was it all happening again? Was the Rebel Alliance just another doomed resistance? Were Luke and Leia marked for death, or worse?

No, Ferus thought, stepping into the Rebel briefing room, readying himself to face the Rebel leadership. *It's different this time. It has to be.* Two decades earlier, a preliminary version of the Death Star had destroyed the kernels of a resistance movement — and nearly everyone Ferus trusted and valued.

But *this* time, Luke had destroyed the Death Star.

The tables were turning. Ferus and Obi-Wan had waited a long time. But Ferus sensed that their wait was almost at an end. He knew well that what felt like instinct could easily be wishful thinking, desire overwhelming good sense. But nonetheless, he needed to believe that this time, they would win.

They would survive.

The Rebel leaders sat at a long table, watching him expectantly: General Rieekan, General Dodonna, Wedge Antilles. Luke, flanked by Leia and his friend Han. Ferus had watched carefully as Leia saw Luke, safe and sound, for the first time. He saw the tears of relief welling in her eyes, and noticed how quickly and surely she wiped them away. He saw that she was still reluctant to leave Luke's side, as if determined to keep him safe, no matter what it took.

They deserve to know, he thought. *Orphaned children,*

alone in the galaxy. They deserve to know they are family.

But even without the truth, it was obvious they still had each other. Some part of them must have known the truth.

Div slouched against a wall in the back of the room. Ferus had requested his presence, and the Rebel leaders had agreed. Div had been slightly harder to convince. But in the end, he had stayed.

"I've spent the last two months tracking Darth Vader's actions," Ferus explained to the assembled group. It had been a difficult task. If he ventured too near, Vader would surely sense his presence and the game would be up. So he'd shadowed the Dark Lord from afar, searching desperately for some clue to his agenda — and some way to foil it. He'd arrived on the Star Destroyer in a TIE fighter equipped with an illegal hyperdrive — his escape route. Keeping the elaborate modifications secret meant keeping the TIE under his sole control. This was the only reason he'd made sure to be behind the controls when the fighters were scrambled. If he hadn't been there, Luke would have flown straight into the Empire's arms. Only luck had saved him. And they couldn't count on luck to do it again. "And among other things, I've learned that Vader has become very interested in an Imperial commander named Rezi Soresh."

"I've never heard of him," General Dodonna said.

"Not surprising," Ferus said. "Soresh keeps a low

profile. He's a master bureaucrat — just shuffling flimsiplast, to all appearances. But he's managed to amass a surprising amount of power, and he's ambitious for more. He has a new plan for currying favor with the Emperor: killing the pilot who destroyed the Death Star."

Every head in the room turned toward Luke.

"Soresh is the man who hired the assassin you know as X-7," Ferus continued.

In the back of the room, Div shifted his weight. It was his only reaction to the words. His face remained blank, his eyes facing forward. But Ferus could sense the shame rolling off him in waves. *He told himself he wasn't working for the Empire,* Ferus observed. *He's been lying to himself for too long, and now it hurts to face the truth.*

He would have borne that pain himself if he could have. But it was Div's burden — and it might be exactly what he needed.

"X-7 has dropped off the radar," Ferus continued. "Even Soresh has lost track of him. But Vader is on his tail. He has agents sweeping the galaxy for any record of his attempts on Luke's life, anyone he may have hired . . ."

Now the faces turned to look at Div. Ferus nodded. "Yes. Lune Divinian is Vader's last link to X-7. That Firespray's files contain all the information Vader's agent has been able to collect on X-7. He was on his way to deliver that — and Div — to Vader."

"I don't understand," Leia said. "Why does Vader care what this Soresh is up to? And why is he so determined to find X-7?"

"That's still unclear," Ferus said, although he was increasingly sure he knew exactly what Vader was up to. And it terrified him. According to Ferus's sources, Vader had learned that Luke was the one who'd destroyed the Death Star. He'd made it a priority to hunt down the Rebel pilot himself — and had made it clear to his men that Luke was *not* to be killed.

It sent a chill up Ferus's spine. Because if Vader was keeping Luke alive, it could mean he knew who Luke really was.

And had plans for him.

"What we do know is that X-7, Soresh, and Vader are all bound together — and I believe if we can find X-7 before they do, we might be able to use him."

"We can find him," Luke said confidently. "We just need the right bait. And obviously —"

"No!" Leia exclaimed. She turned to Luke. "It's too dangerous."

"I can handle it, Leia," Luke said, visibly annoyed.

"I'm not saying you can't handle it. I'm saying it's a foolish risk."

"It's a *worthwhile* risk. *You'd* want to do it."

Ferus cut in. "It's the wrong strategy," he explained. "We don't want to draw X-7 into an attack. We certainly don't want to *kill* him."

"Who's *'we'*?" Han drawled. "Because trust me, I want to —"

"As I say, we want to *use* him," Ferus said, pressing on. "The records on the Firespray indicate that X-7 is trying to hunt down traces of his former identity, from before he was inducted into the Imperial assassin program. He remembers none of it, and he's been completely wiped from the system. But what if he *were* to find some clues to his past? And what if those clues gave him reason to despise the Empire as much as we do? What if instead of killing X-7, we could *turn* him to our side — against the Empire?"

General Rieekan shook his head. "Something like that would require extensive access to Imperial computer systems. I'm not sure we have the resources to spare."

Ferus smiled. Little did they know they were looking at one of the best slicers in the galaxy. Long ago, before Alderaan, before he'd turned himself into an invisible man, he'd been a galaxy-class slicer, specializing in creating false identities. "That won't be a problem," Ferus said. "But in my experience —"

"Your experience as a botanist and courtier?" Leia asked, raising her eyebrows.

"I wasn't always a botanist, Your Highness," he said. "I know about creating false pasts, for men who need them. And I can tell you that just as the best lies always contain a kernel of truth, the best false identities are always based on real ones. Especially when time is short. What we need is an identity to appropriate, a man around X-7's age who died or disappeared a decade ago. Just at the moment when X-7 entered the Empire's program. Someone whose entire family was destroyed by the Empire, someone with reason to want revenge. Perhaps someone with a single remaining relative who can fill in a few carefully selected blanks."

"That's a pretty specific order," General Dodonna said.

"Yes," Ferus said evenly, swallowing the emotion that threatened to consume him. "It is."

Div gave him a look of pure disgust. Then he turned his back on the proceedings and left. Ferus had known that Div would catch on.

And he knew that the younger man wouldn't be easily convinced.

"We give X-7 the identity he's looking for," Ferus said, careful not to betray his distress. "We tell him exactly what we want him to hear — and unleash him on the Empire."

"You want to brainwash a brainwashed man?" Leia asked incredulously. "Then turn him into a weapon?"

"He's already been turned into a weapon," Ferus pointed out. "We're just pointing him in the right direction."

Div closed his eyes and tipped his face up to the sun. The chill water of the creek lapped against his bare ankles. The wind whispered through the leaves, making it easy to imagine ghosts peeking through the spindly Massassi branches. But when he opened his eyes, he was totally alone. Just as he wanted it. The clearing was only a kilometer away from the Great Temple that served as the Rebel Base, but the hidden pocket of jungle was so quiet and still he felt like he was the only man on the moon. It was the kind of spot where he could hear himself think.

It was the kind of spot where he could hide forever.

But of course Ferus found him.

Ferus sat beside him, silent. It was another thing that was different about the Jedi after all these years: The Ferus he remembered had been a talkative, joyful man — at least before things had become really bad. Something dark had settled over Ferus after the day he'd watched Darth Vader murder his dearest friend. A shadow across his face, across his heart. In the end, Ferus had fought off the dark side of the Force, and the light had returned to his eyes. But Div wondered if those days had left a permanent scar.

"You can't mean it," Div said finally. "You can't possibly expect that —"

"I do," Ferus said. "I'm sorry."

Div struggled to control his temper. Ferus obviously thought that Div hated him. But that wasn't the case. It was just that seeing Ferus again hurt, and it was a pain he'd tried long and hard to forget. For years, he'd asked himself, *Why couldn't I protect them?* And he'd wondered whether Ferus could have saved them.

But he hadn't been there. And yes, part of him hated Ferus for that. But not as much as he hated himself. For failing.

"I suppose you're going to tell me it's the only option," Div said sourly.

"No." Ferus paused. "Just the best option."

Div exploded. "How is it the best *anything* to abuse Trever's memory like that? And you honestly expect me to go along with it? For what? To help *them*?" He jerked his head at the path that led back to the Rebel barracks. "You think Trever would want that?"

Ferus tilted his head. "Trever risked his life for this cause, time and time again. He died for it." He swallowed hard. "Using his identity in this way . . . it could give his death meaning."

"Nothing can give his death meaning," Div shot back angrily. "All death is meaningless."

"And all life?" Ferus asked mildly. "Is that the next logical conclusion?"

Div didn't respond. He remembered this from his childhood, the Jedi way—small, innocent questions designed to guide you to one big answer. Ferus always liked to claim he wasn't a *real* Jedi—after all, he'd left the order as a teenager, before becoming a Jedi Master. He'd given up that life and spent nearly a decade living as an ordinary man. But from where Div was sitting, Ferus was just like the rest of them—sure of his own wisdom, sure he was right. Full of secrets. Whatever the technicalities, Div thought, Ferus was a Jedi.

It wasn't a compliment.

"This won't work without your cooperation," Ferus said. "But I didn't come out here to convince you." He stood up, brushing the dirt off his clothes. He'd borrowed the ill-fitting shirt from General Dodonna. It was strange to see him dressed as a Rebel soldier—nearly as strange as it had been to see him in Imperial garb. "The choice is yours, Div." He patted Div on the shoulder. And as much as he wanted to, Div didn't squirm away. "I trust you. I always have."

Maybe you shouldn't, Div thought as Ferus left him. *You trusted me to look after Trever, and look how that worked out.*

It had been a long time since anyone had trusted him, and since he'd dared trust anyone else. Trusting people was the kind of thing that got you dead in a hurry. And letting other people trust you was nearly as dangerous. It meant their lives were your responsibility — and so were their deaths. It was easier to be alone.

But once Ferus was gone, Div grew disgusted by his own company. He started back toward the Rebel camp. Midway, Luke appeared, his little astromech droid in tow.

Luke waved, grinning. "Glad I found you!"

"You were looking for me?" Div asked, instantly cautious. The Rebels seemed to have lost interest in locking him up now that they had all the information they needed on this X-7. But Div hadn't forgotten that before that day, he'd been a prisoner on this moon.

And he suspected that Luke hadn't forgotten that Div had once tried to kill him.

Luke drew his lightsaber and activated the beam.

Div tensed, ready to leap out of the way. He'd seen Luke handle the weapon. His efforts were clumsy, hesitant. Div could disarm him. Probably.

"I come out here to practice sometimes," Luke said. "More privacy, you know?"

"Uh, yeah." Div felt like a fool.

"Back on Kamino, you saved my life with this thing," Luke said, lifting the lightsaber. "Like you'd been using it your whole life."

Div shrugged. "Like I say, just something I picked up."

"Well, I was kind of hoping . . ." Luke reddened. "You think you could teach me some moves?"

"What?"

"It's no big deal," Luke said quickly. "I just figured . . . I don't really have anyone else who can show me how to use this thing."

That's what you think, Div thought. He didn't understand why Ferus was so determined not to tell Luke the truth. Why not start training him as a Jedi *now,* before it was too late?

Like it's too late for me.

"Sounds great," Div said. "I could use the exercise."

It wasn't exercise he needed. It was distraction. Pushing himself to the point of exhaustion, and past it. This was perfect.

"Think of the lightsaber as an extension of your body," he said, repeating the advice he'd been given by the Jedi Ry-Gaul and Garen Muln. "Always be aware of its position, but never watch your blade — you watch your *enemy.* Your focus has to be narrow and wide, all at once."

Div showed him Shii-Cho, the first of the seven Jedi fighting forms. He taught Luke the basics, thrust and parry, lunge and deflect. Div cringed as Luke ran through his velocity drills looking like a child waving a stick. But he would learn. Form III, Soresu, was more advanced, but Luke had already figured out many of the basic laserblast-deflection techniques. His movements were still too loose and ranging, making him a wide target for incoming blasts.

Every time Div used the lightsaber to demonstrate, it was more difficult to hand it back. His body remembered all the moves, effortlessly falling into old habits. But it wasn't just the fighting techniques, or the deadly efficiency of the blade.

A lightsaber wasn't just another weapon. Using it, even for practice, meant connecting with the Force. There was no other way to achieve the balance, the necessary equilibrium of stillness and motion. Wielding the lightsaber meant opening himself up to everything he'd shut out these last several years. It meant unlocking a door in his mind that he'd thought was sealed forever.

It was tempting to believe that it wasn't. Ferus seemed to believe that Luke could begin his training even as an adult — contrary to everything Div knew about Jedi traditions. So why couldn't Div return to his training, reclaim the skills of his youth, fulfill the destiny everyone had foreseen for him?

Even if he'd wanted it, Div felt sure it wouldn't work. Being a Jedi meant opening oneself up to the Force. It meant having trust. It required a degree of blind faith, of innocence, that Div had long since lost the capability to feel. He wasn't willing to let that vulnerability — that *weakness* — back into himself.

"Like this?" Luke asked, executing a perfect riposte-counterparry combination. He spun around, bouncing lightly on the balls of his feet, slashing the light-saber across a bough of the nearest Massassi tree with startling accuracy. Not that Div was about to reveal that he was impressed.

"That's great . . . as long as your enemy moves no faster than a tree," Div said. "Again!"

Luke swept through the training exercise again, and again, blade flashing, eyes lit with determination. Div couldn't help remembering his own training, many years ago. Hiding out on an asteroid with all those proud warriors, so eager for the day when he would be big enough to fight by their side. They had died for him, all of them. Gave him their one escape pod. Watched him disappear into space and waited to die. Safe in his pod, Div had watched as the Imperials had aimed their terrible weapon at the asteroid and erased it from existence.

All those people, giving up their lives so that Div could escape — so that the galaxy's "only hope" would survive.

All that, and it wasn't me after all, Div thought as Luke slashed and leapt and spun, striving for perfection. *But what if it's him?*

Belazura was a sewer.

According to the records, the planet had once been a popular vacation spot, its long stretches of white sandy beaches calling tourists from all over the Inner Rim. X-7 had scanned the holopics in disgust. All that land, wasted on useless pursuits. Pale bodies stretching out under the three suns. Children splashing in the surf. And behind them, acres of lush green hills, cluttered with roaming herds of wilter-beasts and hairy bronaks.

The inefficiency of it was criminal — or should have been, at least.

X-7 climbed out of his Howlrunner and looked around with satisfaction. It was an open-air spaceport, left over from the old days, when it would have afforded views of the sparkling coastlines and blooming hills. Those were all gone now, thanks to the Empire. The hills had been stripped as 11-17 miner droids probed the earth beneath for valuable varmigio and mutonium. Derricks and power generators dotted the water as far as the eye could see. The water itself had turned nearly black with runoff from the factories lining the coast; the three suns were barely visible through the thick haze of brown smog. X-7 took a deep, appreciative breath. That foul stench was the perfume of civilization.

The people of Belazura had plenty to thank the Empire for. Before the Imperials arrived, Belazurans had been useless fools whose skills were limited to serving tropical drinks and pulling flailing Phindians out of the surf. But the Empire had put them to work in the mines and the factories, turned them into productive galactic citizens.

Though none of them looked very happy about it.

Except for periodic convoys of Imperial troop carriers, the narrow streets of Belazura's capital city were nearly deserted. Small wonder, as every able-bodied man and woman was either at work or asleep. But those who couldn't work — the aged, the infirm, the very young — shuffled down the sidewalks, heads down, shoulders hunched. X-7 had no hope that anyone here would recognize him from his past; Project Omega had rebuilt his facial structure. But even if he'd worn the same face as this Trever Flume, there seemed little chance that any of these Belazurans would even dare look at him.

X-7 had followed the trail of information as far as it would take him. It had taken him here. Soresh's codes had provided access to an encrypted Imperial network that had revealed all he could ever want to know about Project Omega. How its unwilling recruits were culled from prisoners whose families thought they were dead. How their brains were wiped. How they were molded into slaves of the Empire, convinced that they had been volunteers. How the records of their past were wiped from the system.

But information wasn't nearly as easy to erase as most people thought. It had been well buried, but X-7 had found it — little more than a name, Trever Flume. Captured on Belazura at age eighteen, shipped off to Project Omega, where he became its most successful graduate. Code name: X-7.

That was it, the dead end. So X-7 had stolen himself a Howlrunner and flown to Belazura. He wasn't leaving until he'd found some answers.

The simplest way to track down information would have been to report to the Imperial liaison at the spaceport. But X-7 needed to stay off the Imperial radar. And likely some kind of fail-safe trigger in the system existed, designed to red-flag anyone who came looking for answers about Trever Flume.

Instead, he decided to begin his search for the past in a more obvious place: Trever Flume's home.

My home? he wondered, staring at the decrepit, crumbling structure that had been Flume's last known address. The two-story house was falling apart: peeling paint, rusted siding, broken generator. Its windows were boarded up, Rebel graffiti scrawled across them in fading reds and blues. It was abandoned; that was clear.

X-7 closed his eyes, trying to force a memory. But the flashbacks always came when he least expected and least desired them. When he was *trying* to remember, his mind stayed blank.

"You don't belong around here."

X-7 whirled around, furious with himself that he hadn't heard the Arconan approaching. By instinct, his hand flashed toward his blaster — but he stopped himself. The Arconan's anvil-shaped head was shriveled with age, his marble-like eyes milky and unfocused. Despite his hostile glare, there was no chance he'd be a threat. *Let it play out,* X-7 thought. *I can always kill him later.*

He adopted a mild, harmless expression. Project Omega might have stripped him of the ability to *experience* human emotion, but he was remarkably good at imitating it. "I'm looking for the family that used to live here," he said. "They're old friends of mine, and since I'm passing through town, I thought I'd catch up."

The Arconan looked around at the crumbling buildings and cratered street. "No one just *passes through* this part of town."

Patience, X-7 cautioned himself, itching for his blaster.

He'd make this being talk, one way or another. But it would be smartest to do so without attracting unwanted attention. The street might be empty, but he could see plenty of windows with a perfect view. Anyone could be lurking behind the transparisteel.

"I'm in Belazura on business, and—"

"Imperial business?" the Arconan said, now even more suspicious. "Haven't you people done enough? What now? You want to torture their ghosts?"

"Does that mean you knew them?" X-7 asked eagerly. "The Flumes?"

"What's it to you?"

"I told you, I'm an old friend."

The Arconan sneered. "Right. An old friend who came by to say hello after all these years. Except I tell you they're dead and you don't even blink. So how about you tell me what you *really* want?"

"Money," X-7 said without hesitation. "What else does anyone want?"

"They owe you?" the Arconan asked.

"Big-time."

The Arconan made a strange sound, like a dianoga choking on a lump of sewage. X-7 suddenly realized he was laughing. "Good luck getting them to pay you back now!" he chortled. But quickly, he sobered up. "You want some help tracking down what's left of Flume's people? It's going to cost you."

Again, X-7 swallowed his irritation. This Arconan didn't know how close he was to death. "How much?"

"Fifty."

"Twenty," X-7 countered.

"Fifty."

"Thirty," X-7 offered.

"Fifty."

He was too impatient to negotiate. Money was nothing to him. He threw a handful of it at the alien. "That's half. Give me the address, and I'll hand over the other half."

The Arconan complied, giving him an address on the fringes of town.

"If this information is inaccurate, I'll be back for you," X-7 said coolly. Now he finally withdrew the blaster from its holster.

"Oh, it's accurate," the alien said, laughing again. "You'll find what's left of them, for all the good it will do you."

X-7 wasn't looking to do himself good. He was looking for answers. After that, who knew? Maybe he would reclaim his old identity and learn to be human again, weak and pathetic.

Or maybe he would track down every last Flume, kill them all, and be done with this mess forever.

The rest of them, X-7 thought sourly. *Perfect.*

The Arconan hadn't lied. Not technically, at least.

Presumably whatever was left of Trever Flume's family was here — underground. Beneath the crooked tombstones. At the edge of an old graveyard, weeds spouting between the mounds of dirt.

Trever Flume.

Clive Flax.

Astri Divinian.

They didn't share a name, but the epitaphs — *loving brother, loving mother, loving father* — made it clear they were a family. *Love.* It put a bad taste in his mouth.

There was something about the last name *Divinian.* Something familiar. Could it mean he was on the right track? X-7 stared at the graves, trying to feel something. "My parents," he said aloud, testing the phrase on his tongue. It felt wrong.

"Trever," he tried next. "My name is Trever."

Each of the three graves had *"Gone never. Here forever,"* the standard Belazuran mourning cry, etched across the top.

Each was marked by a bouquet of nahtival flowers. The flowers were fresh; *someone* was tending to these graves.

X-7 paced quickly to the entrance of the graveyard, where a hunched Belazuran had been hacking at the ground with a rusty shovel. He was still there, now sliding a tombstone into the shallow hole.

"Who's been here today?" X-7 asked harshly.

The weary Belazuran looked at him blankly.

"Today!" X-7 shouted. "Someone put fresh flowers on those graves." He gestured toward the Divinian plots. "Who was it?"

The man nodded slowly. "That's right, he did come by today. Didn't expect him."

X-7 grabbed the man's shoulders and gave him a brutal shake. "Him *who*, you mudcrutch?"

"The boy," the man said in a dreamy voice. "Of course, he's not a boy anymore, is he? Time's passing, it is. Slow, fast, it just keeps going. Yesterday we're a republic, today we're an empire, tomorrow—"

"The boy," X-7 growled.

"A man now," the Belazuran said. "Thought I wouldn't recognize him, but I did, didn't I? Looks just like his mother. Astri was a beauty, that one."

So Trever had a brother. There had been a suspicious lack of information about Trever's family in the files, as if it had been purposefully blotted out. But this was better than a file; this was a living relative, in the flesh. In reach. *If* the man could focus long enough to spill the details. *He'll tell me what I need*, X-7 thought with determination. *Even if I have to cut it out of him.*

"Lucky boy," the old man said. "Don't know why he doesn't spend more time in that house. Not many lucky enough to have an ocean view, not these days."

"I was just at Flume's house," X-7 snapped. "No one's living there. It's falling apart."

"Falling apart?" The man shook his head. "It was fine yesterday, in perfect condition. Perfect condition the day before. Walk past it every day on my way home, I do. Don't know why they kept it as a summerhouse. If it were my house, I'd live in it year-round, day in, day out, I would. But not them. Two months a year, in and out. Never made much sense to me."

"Where is it?" X-7 asked harshly. "Where's this summerhouse?"

The grave tender narrowed his eyes, suddenly suspicious. "Why do *you* want to know?"

X-7 sighed. Of course the senile Belazuran chose *now* to come out of his daze. X-7 didn't have the patience for deception or persuasion. He lashed out with lightning speed, grabbing the man by the neck. Then he squeezed. "Tell me where the house is. Or die."

The man gasped, trying desperately to draw in breath. His hands hammered at X-7's arm, but the blows were as negligible as tesfli piercer bites. "Time's running out," X-7 said. "I'm sure I can obtain the information somewhere else — but I won't be very happy about it." He squeezed tighter.

The man's eyes bulged. He wheezed something inaudible.

"What's that?" X-7 relaxed his grip very slightly.

"The Fallows, beyond the city, along the water. The blue house, you can't miss it," he gasped. "Please. Please don't kill me."

It would take minimal effort to squeeze just a bit tighter, to cut off the man's air entirely. That way he wouldn't be able to tell anyone about the strange man who'd come around asking questions; he wouldn't be able to warn the brother. It made sense. That was the rule: When in doubt, kill.

But he didn't do it. Something strange stilled his hand. *Mercy?*

The thought repulsed him. Enraged, he slammed a fist into the grave tender's head, hard enough to guarantee he wouldn't be warning anyone anytime soon. The grave tender crumpled to the ground. And X-7 set off in search of his past.

He scaled the exterior of the house and perched on a ledge beside a large picture window. The ledge was only a few centimeters wide, but he was in no danger of losing his balance. The fogged transparisteel offered an imperfect view of the living room. But he could make out the figure puttering around inside. He could have just knocked on the door. But he was no fool. If this was a trap, he wasn't about to walk straight into it. Recon first, then action.

The man kept his face away from the window.

Turn around, X-7 ordered him silently. *Show me who you are.*

As if in reaction to the silent command, the man turned. X-7 stiffened in surprise. He'd seen that face before. Not in a half-remembered flash of childhood. Less than a month before, on an arid moon, accepting a mission to kill Luke Skywalker. The man was a mercenary pilot, one of the best, by the name of Lune —

Divinian! he suddenly remembered. As in *Astri* Divinian. It wasn't like him to forget those kinds of details. That was the sort of mistake that could get you killed. The sort of mistake that would lead you straight into a trap.

Because the odds against that man being his brother? Astronomical. There was a much more likely possibility.

X-7 gritted his teeth, furious that he'd allowed himself to be misled. This Divinian obviously had some kind of ax to grind. Perhaps he was still angry to have lost out on his payment when the Kamino mission went sour. Whatever the reason, he'd decided to come after X-7. To play with his mind, his emotions.

Bad mistake.

Recon was over, X-7 decided. Time for action.

He hurled himself through the window. Lune Divinian flung his hands over his face, shielding himself from the hail of transparisteel. And all traces of mercy wiped away, X-7 lunged for his throat.

The thunder of stormtrooper boots was growing louder, closer. Han dragged Leia around the corner, but the corridor dead-ended a few meters away. No cover, no escape. They pressed themselves against the wall, held their breath, and hoped.

A phalanx of stormtroopers stomped down the hallway, feet rising and falling in unison. As they swept past, Han whispered into the comlink, cupping his hands around it to block the noise. "A little more warning next time?"

"It's all clear now," Luke's voice assured him. "You have a straight shot to the records room. Two guards at the door, and you're in. Easy."

"Sure, easy for *you*," Han muttered. "You're not the one in here making friends with the boys in white."

"What's that?"

"Nothing, kid. In and out. We'll get those blueprints to you faster than a neek." Han glowered at the comlink.

Bad enough he was infiltrating an Imperial administrative center with only the kid's help to guide him through. Even worse that Leia had insisted on coming, too. Which meant that if there was trouble — make that *when* there was trouble — he couldn't just save his own neck. He'd have to save hers, too. It was his responsibility.

Except none of this is my responsibility, he thought irritably. *So what am I doing here?*

Div had agreed to go along with Ferus's plan, but he'd demanded something in return: a Rebel attack on Belazura's Imperial garrison. The garrison was the center of Imperial power on the planet, but it was also a valuable strategic asset for the Empire. At the heart of the Inner Rim, it gave them a perfect base to control the surrounding planetary systems. Dark rumors swirled about the weaponry housed there. Belazura was packed with Imperial factories and arms manufactures, and several of the latest prototypes were said to be stored in the garrison. It was one of the reasons the citizens of Belazura were thoroughly cowed by their Imperial rulers. And one of the reasons it had long sat toward the top of the Rebels' target list.

The garrison was built on the spot where Div's entire family had died.

So Han understood why Div wanted it gone. He knew why the Rebels had decided to go along with Div and plan a strike. He was less clear about why he'd agreed to go along, much less volunteered for this recon mission.

The garrison's blueprints were considered so valuable that they weren't stored in the computer system. Instead, only one hard copy existed, and it was housed in the basement of the Imperial administration center. Leia had appointed herself the one to retrieve it.

So here he was, by her side.

Han wasn't a big fan of whys. It didn't matter *why* he was here. All that mattered was getting in, getting the blueprints, and getting out. Both of them.

"Luke says go now," he told Leia. R2-D2 had managed to tap into the security systems. He'd disabled the security alerts and holocams. Now Luke could see what was happening inside the building, but he was the only one. Luke was monitoring from beyond the perimeter, guiding them through safely. Supposedly.

Han and Leia ran soundlessly down the corridor, turning right at the third corner. And as promised, only two stormtroopers stood guarding the door. They fumbled with their blasters as Han and Leia appeared in the hallway.

But Han was faster. Laserfire burst from his blaster, and the stormtrooper on the right went down. The other dropped at nearly the same instant. Leia pocketed her smoking blaster pistol. Han shook his head in appreciation. The princess might have an attitude — but she also had perfect aim.

"Ready?" Leia asked, preparing the detonite charge that would blow open the locked door.

Han nodded and raised his blaster. There were no security holocams in the basement records room, which meant they were going in blind. He was ready, all right. Ready for anything.

Except for the door exploding *out* toward them before Leia even had a chance to plant the charge. Han and Leia flew backward, slamming hard into the wall. Their blasters clattered out of their hands.

Han lifted himself up. He shook his head and blinked hard, hoping he was seeing double. Maybe triple.

But the vision was real. A line of stormtroopers emerged from the dark basement and opened fire.

"Han!" Luke shouted into the comlink, starting to panic. "Leia! Han! What's going on?" But the comlink broadcast nothing but shouting and explosions. Luke was certain that amid the chaos, he heard Leia scream.

"Chewie! Come on — we're going in!" Luke cried, already springing into motion. He'd been monitoring the mission from a hidden spot by the freight entrance while Chewbacca waited nearby with the landspeeder, ready to take off at a moment's notice. The Wookiee didn't hesitate.

He threw himself against the door, which gave way like it was made of flimsiplast. Luke and Chewbacca barreled down the hallway. Luke led the way, the building's twisting corridors engraved in his mind. Not that it was difficult to find their way to the basement; all they had to do was follow the noise. Laserfire pings, shouts, grunts, explosions, and, again, something that sounded terrifyingly like Leia's scream.

They rounded the corner. Stormtrooper bodies littered the corridor. Han and Leia were battling their way through a storm of plastoid armor and laserfire. Smoke billowed through the hallway, giving their faces a gray, sickly pallor. Han aimed his weapon at one of the stormtroopers, but nothing happened. Luke realized he was out of ammo.

"Han, heads up!" he shouted, and without thinking, tossed his blaster over to his friend. Han jumped up and snatched it out of the air, then began firing again before his feet touched the ground.

Chewbacca's bowcaster was of little use in such a cramped space, but the Wookiee didn't hesitate to charge into the fight. He grabbed the stormtrooper closest to Leia and twisted his blaster into a knot with one hand as he slammed the trooper against the wall with the other.

Luke took it all in, even as he tried desperately to disarm the stormtroopers with his lightsaber. *Loose grip, firm shoulders, don't lean too hard to the right,* he thought, trying to remember all the advice Div had given him. He bent his knees slightly and tried to remember the first form — but was he supposed to parry before thrust, or thrust before parry? A blast of laserfire whizzing past his ear knocked him out of his confusion. *Stop trying to be a Jedi warrior,* he told himself. *Just stay alive.* Forgetting about form and technique and strategy, he hacked blindly with the lightsaber, letting the glowing blade guide his hands. The stormtrooper dropped to the ground.

Yes! Luke thought. Then he saw Han standing behind the fallen trooper, a smoking blaster in his hands. "Thanks for the loaner," he said, hoisting it at Luke like he was toasting a glass of lum. "Consider us even."

It was the last of the stormtroopers. But surely more would be on the way. While Leia and Chewbacca covered the corridor, Luke and Han raced down into the records room. They tore through the files, searching for the garrison blueprints. Finally, Han shouted in triumph. "Got it!" he said, brandishing a data chip. "Let's go."

They ran up the steps. Once at the top, Luke tossed a fragmentation grenade into the records room and slammed the door behind it. A moment later, they heard a muffled explosion. The Imperials would know they'd been here — but they would never know what the Rebels were trying to steal.

Footsteps pounded down the hallway. Their time was up. Luke led the way out of the building, but when they broke through to open air, they stopped cold.

Their landspeeder was gone.

"This way!" Luke shouted, catching sight of a few Imperial scout speeder bikes parked nearby. They raced toward them.

"Stop right there, you Rebel scum!" a stormtrooper shouted.

Laserfire shot past them. Running flat out toward the bikes, Luke twisted around and fired over his shoulder. The stormtrooper dived for cover. A second one had joined him, a blaster rifle in each hand.

Chewbacca reached the speeder bikes first and looked at them dubiously. They were narrow repulsorlift vehicles designed for a single rider. Handlebars for steering, foot pedals for speed and altitude, and no margin for error. The Wookiee growled something at Han, waving his furry arms in the air. Han shoved him toward the closest bike. "It'll hold you," Han said quickly. "Trust me." He hopped onto one of his own and lifted off. The Wookiee let out a mournful sigh, but he trusted Han. He jumped onto the bike and started the engine. It wobbled slightly, its repulsorlifts struggling to support the Wookiee's weight, but then the engine roared and the bike shot forward.

There was only one bike left.

"I said *stop*!" the stormtrooper shouted.

"I'll drive," Leia said, yanking Luke toward the bike. "You shoot."

They climbed on together and lifted off, thrusters on full. Luke straddled the bike and wrapped one arm around Leia's waist, using the other to fire back at the stormtroopers, who were fumbling with the door of a small storage shed off the side of the main administrative building.

Luke quickly understood why. The shed contained more speeder bikes. The stormtroopers were giving chase.

"Faster!" Luke urged Leia. "We have to get out of here!"

"Gee, thanks for the great idea," Leia drawled. But the bike accelerated. The city turned into a grayish smear as they sped away from the dense center and out toward the corridor of factories along the coastline. Luke turned back and fired another barrage of laserfire. The stormtroopers swooped out of the way. One of them veered straight into the path of an oncoming troop carrier. It exploded on impact.

Luke grabbed Leia tighter as the shock wave slammed into them. The bike lurched forward and dropped several feet. Luke's stomach rocketed into his throat. But he kept firing. And Leia never flinched at the controls. She made a sharp turn into a narrow passageway, trying to lose the remaining stormtrooper in a zigzag of alleys. But the bike behind them drew closer and closer, and Leia had pushed the thrusters as far as they would go. They shot toward a narrow spit of land bounded by sea on one side and by a murky bay of toxic runoff from the nearby factories on the other.

The stormtrooper fired his bike's blaster cannon. The beam of laserfire pinged off the main battery of Luke's speeder. The speeder shuddered and lurched precariously to the side. Luke, who was holding on with only one hand, lost his balance. The bike tilted further, dumping him off the seat. He scrabbled for purchase but felt himself slipping. They weren't very high off the ground, but if he hit at this speed . . . He was dangling half off the bike, and as it tipped further, he lost his grip completely.

"Hold on!" Leia shouted, grasping his hand.

Luke dangled in midair. She couldn't hoist him up, not with one hand. It was hard enough to steer while holding on to him. And impossible to fire at the approaching stormtrooper.

Desperate, Luke had an idea. "Fly over the bay!" Luke shouted up to her, hoping she'd hear him over the roar of the engines. He held tight as she steered toward the toxic water. He winced as his body slammed into the bike, buffeted by the wind. They were flying so low that his toes skimmed the water. There was a sizzling noise and a trail of smoke as the toxic liquid ate away at his shoe. Luke yanked his legs out of the way and gripped Leia's hand tighter. He tried not to look down.

He still had his blaster, which meant he had a chance. Wind tore at his body, trying to rip it from Leia's grip. The stormtrooper was firing relentlessly, his shots coming closer and closer to the mark. He didn't have much time. And it was nearly impossible to aim, dangling by one hand as he shot forward at two hundred kilometers an hour.

But Luke was sure of one thing: He could hit any target at any speed. He blocked out the wind, the bubbling toxic sludge, the hail of laserfire.

He squeezed the trigger.

Direct hit. The Imperial's primary drive motor exploded in a shower of sparks, and the bike began spinning out of control. The stormtrooper went flying into the soupy lake of toxic waste. He landed with a loud splash, thrashing and flailing in the bubbling iridescent water. But soon he slipped below, the white armor disappearing into the deep. Luke shuddered.

A few more seconds, a little less luck, and it could have been him.

Leia helped him climb back aboard the bike. The engine thrummed beneath him. Leia was shaking. Luke took a deep breath, steadying himself. "Let's go," he suggested, trying his best not to look at the toxic soup swirling beneath him. "Meet up with the others and start planning phase two."

"Let's just hope it goes better than phase one," Leia said, turning toward the rendezvous point.

"Couldn't go worse," Luke pointed out.

Leia twisted around to give him a wry smile. "You know what Han would say to that."

Luke was pretty sure he did. And he had to admit, for once, the pilot was probably right. "Things can always get worse."

X-7 closed his fingers around the enemy's neck and squeezed. He would throttle the life out of this imposter. Punish him for daring to believe he could fool X-7. That level of idiocy deserved death. Div gasped for air as red bloomed across his cheeks — blood vessels, bursting in the struggle for oxygen.

The enemy jerked his hands up in a reverse Moravian maneuver. X-7 toppled backward, and the enemy was on him in a heartbeat. They rolled across the carpet, knocking over a synthstone table. Dishes and glasses clattered to the ground, shattering on impact. X-7 raised an arm to protect himself against the spray of jagged fragments. But his enemy grabbed a wrist and flipped X-7 onto his back.

As he fell, X-7 hooked his leg behind his foe's and brought him down, too. But the enemy had seen the move coming, and grabbed a fire poker from the fireplace on his way down. He slammed the durasteel rod down at X-7's face.

X-7 rolled out of the way just in time. He drew his blaster. With lightning speed, the enemy knocked it out of his hand. It skidded across the room, disappearing under a couch.

The enemy was a blur with the poker, lashing and lunging like a master swordsman. Driven by instinct, X-7 reached blindly, his hands closing around a curtain rod and ripping it off the wall. Some part of him must have noticed it earlier and filed it away for later use. That was why X-7 was invincible. He fought like a machine. No emotion, no passion. Only speed and observation and power. He moved with grace and without hesitation. He was like a force of nature. He had been bred for battle. He was a deadly weapon.

And yet the enemy matched him. Move for move.

Their makeshift weapons clashed and clanged. X-7 launched an attack, but the enemy countered with a Phr'shan maneuver. A Griggs-Barnay was the next logical move, but instead, X-7 opted for the unexpected, slashing at the enemy with a modified Ptann attack that he had picked up on Tarivo III. The enemy danced backward almost before X-7 had begun to strike, as if he knew what X-7 was going to do even before X-7 himself did.

They were too evenly matched. X-7 needed to regain

the advantage. He began consciously to speed up his breathing, as if he were struggling for air. Sweat streamed down his face. "Hold," he gasped, panting. He let the enemy take the offensive and back him further and further across the room. "We need to talk."

The enemy lashed out with the poker. X-7 parried the blow but let his arm sag just a bit. He didn't want to look *too* weak. Just weak enough that it would be believable for him to stop the fight.

"You break into *my* home, attack me without cause or warning, and you expect *me* to take pity on you?" the enemy growled. He pounced on X-7, who shifted his weight and leaned into the attack, using the enemy's momentum to throw him halfway across the room.

"Not pity," X-7 said, dropping into a crouch behind the sofa. His blaster was under there somewhere. If he could just reach it . . . "But if you're at all curious why I'm here . . ."

There! His hand closed around the blaster. He lodged it into his belt, tucking it beneath his shirt. Then he stood again, arms out to his sides. "A temporary ceasefire, that's all I'm suggesting. Time for explanations."

The enemy took a few cautious steps toward him, the fire poker lowered to his side. He nodded. "Fine. Explanations. You start."

X-7 could tell when a man's defenses were dropped. It was a predator's instinct, knowing exactly when to strike.

"My pleasure," he said. Then raised the blaster, squeezed the trigger, and—

Somehow, the enemy wasn't there anymore. The blasterfire blew a hole in the wall. A cold blade pressed against X-7's neck. Warm blood trickled down his skin. The enemy was behind him.

The enemy had proven faster than him. Stronger than him. Smarter than him.

There was a chance he could dislodge the knife, knock the enemy off balance, disarm him, all before the knife plunged deeper and sliced an artery.

X-7 closed his eyes, let the blaster drop to the ground, and waited for the end. He had been bested, and it was no less than he deserved.

But the pressure of the knife dropped away. "*Now* perhaps you're ready to explain what you're doing here."

X-7 whirled around, ready to strike, but the enemy caught his arm before a blow could fall.

"Talk," Lune Divinian said.

It was his only viable option. He wouldn't risk hand-to-hand combat again, not until he found a way to regain the advantage. "Did you really think I would fall for it?" X-7 snarled. "Believe a man like you could be my *brother*?"

The man visibly recoiled. "My brother is dead."

"Your adopted brother, you mean," X-7 said, correcting him.

It was like the man's face turned to durasteel. His expression went completely blank. "What do you know about it?"

There was something strangely familiar about the dull eyes, the toneless voice, but it took X-7 a moment to pin it down. Then he realized that it was the same blank and pitiless gaze he saw in the mirror. This was the only man he'd ever met who was able to shut himself down as completely as X-7.

Just as he was the only man X-7 had ever met who could so evenly match him, strength for strength, move to move.

Is it possible . . . ?

"I know everything about it," X-7 said, "but that's just what you intended, isn't it? Planted the information for me to find, invented this ridiculous story. You probably didn't even have a brother. This person, this *Trever*—"

Lune Divinian struck him across the face. Hard.

X-7 forced himself not to respond.

"You don't say his name," Lune said. "Ever."

It didn't make sense. If this was all a trap and Lune was behind it, then wouldn't he be welcoming X-7 with open arms? Certainly he could be lying, trying to put X-7 off balance, confuse him. But X-7 had never met the man who could successfully lie to him. People were too emotional, too invested in their own words. X-7 was separate from all that, separate from humanity. The distance allowed him to see behind people's masks, into the rotting truth that lay beneath. And he didn't think that Lune was lying.

He *thought* Lune was telling the truth, but didn't *know*. Wasn't *certain*.

Before, he would have been. Uncertainty wasn't a part of his programming.

Of course, neither was memory. Or curiosity. Or anger.

But X-7 wasn't the man he had once been.

It was proving to be a problem.

Div let X-7 think it took him some convincing. He looked through X-7's evidence, challenging his story at every turn. Refused to accept that Trever might be alive, standing in front of him.

And then, on the third day, he did. And in the process, X-7 accepted it, too.

Now Div couldn't decide where to rest his eyes. Not on the familiar threadbare couch, a hole on its armrest torn long ago by Trever's rambunctious pet bull worrt. Not on the door to the kitchen, where Astri had so often appeared with a pot of some foul-smelling concoction. She had always tried to recreate her father's recipes, but more times than not, her efforts had resulted in an inedible sludge. Clive had eaten it anyway, a smile fixed on his face. (Apparently love wasn't just blind; it was taste bud–deprived.) But at Trever's suggestion, Div had devised a better system: dumping the sludge into their napkins, then using the Force to float it out of sight.

Div couldn't look at the empty desk that had once been covered by Astri's computer clutter, or the shelves that had once been filled with Clive's collection of exotic Merenzane Gold vintages. The caretaker who came in once a month had managed to keep the abandoned house from falling in on itself, but she couldn't stop the dust from collecting. She couldn't turn the house back into a home.

She couldn't clear out the ghosts.

It had been a week. And with each passing day, it grew easier to see those ghosts; it became harder to forget. Which was why he almost couldn't bear to look around the house. But anything would be easier than looking at X-7, who was sitting on Trever's couch, wearing Trever's clothes, flipping through Trever's old collection of Gravball trading cards.

X-7 tossed them onto a side table. "I don't understand," he said. "Why would he . . . I . . . anyone collect something with no value?"

"For fun," Div said. "It made you happy."

X-7 riffled through a stack of holopics sitting on the table. He picked up one of Trever grinning in front of a shiny new Arrow-23 speeder. It had been his fifteenth birthday. "Happy." X-7 frowned and shook his head. "I can't remember that."

It wasn't the only thing he and Div had in common.

There were their strength and agility, of course, and their single-minded determination. But it wasn't just that. They were both men without a past. They understood each other.

"Tell me again," X-7 said. "Tell me how it happened."

Div sighed. He'd told so many stories of the past, but this was the only one X-7 ever wanted to hear.

"They were betrayed," Div said. "It was supposed to be a simple raid. The munitions factory should have been an easy target. But one of the Rebels sold them out to the Empire . . . stormtroopers everywhere. They . . . they never had a chance."

"They killed our parents," X-7 said, brushing his fingers across a holopic of Astri. "Except they weren't really my parents."

"They were. In every way that counted," Div said fiercely.

"But Trever —"

"You," Div said, correcting him. "You managed to sneak into the factory."

"You were watching from the ridge, with electrobinocs," X-7 said. "You were too far away. Too young."

"You saw Astri and Clive go down," Div said. "You still had the charges, and you were determined to get them inside. You weren't about to let them die in vain. But then . . ." He shook his head. "I still don't understand it."

"Then the TIE fighters dropped the concussion missiles," X-7 finished for him. "They destroyed their own factory. With me inside."

"They killed our people for trying to destroy it — and then they blew it up," Div said. It was the one thing he'd never been able to understand. It made all the death even more pointless.

"Because you've never worked with the Empire," X-7 said. "It's obvious: They have something they couldn't risk falling into Rebel hands. Or maybe they were planning on razing it anyway, to build the garrison — so they destroyed it before you could. To make a point."

"A point that killed hundreds of their own men," Div said.

"Men are expendable," X-7 said with chilling calm. Then he gave himself a small shake. "I mean, that's what the Empire believes. That's what the Rebels don't understand."

Div understood. As soon as he'd seen that laserfire blast Astri to the ground, he'd understood.

"Except, they didn't kill everyone inside the factory," Div said. "There were survivors. You."

X-7 became very still. His face was a chalky gray. He looked up from the holopics and, for the first time in a week, met Div's eyes. "I may have made it out of that factory alive. But, Div, we both have to accept it: Your brother did not survive. Whoever I was, it's not . . . we can't . . ."

Hesitantly, half afraid he'd end up shot in the head, Div put a hand on X-7's shoulder. "You're here now," Div said. "So maybe we can."

"You're late," Ferus said as Div arrived at the rendezvous point. Div and Trever had discovered the abandoned shack, a few kilometers from the house, many years earlier. They'd once used it as a clubhouse, where Trever pretended to be interested in Div's childish games, because that was what brothers did. Even adopted brothers. As they'd grown older, it had become a useful meeting point for the Belazuran resistance.

"It's not easy," Div said. "He's watching me all the time."

"I'm sorry you have to go through this," Ferus said. "If I could bear it for you —"

Div shook his head. "It's fine. It's actually . . ."

"What?"

"Nothing."

But Ferus looked at him with those placid, knowing eyes, and Div couldn't help continuing. "Whoever X-7 was, he was conscripted into Project Omega against his will. We know that. Brainwashed to forget whoever he used to be. He must have had a family, people who missed him — who may think he's dead. So isn't it possible . . ." Div was too ashamed to say it out loud. As he put the hope into words, even he could see how ludicrous it was.

"Possible that Trever is still alive somewhere?" Ferus said sadly. "Possible, even, that our lie has stumbled upon the truth? That X-7 really is —"

"I never said that," Div cut in harshly. "I'm no fool."

"A coincidence like that —"

"Aren't you Jedi always saying there *are* no coincidences?" Div asked.

"I would know if it was Trever," Ferus said heavily. "I would sense it."

"But I wouldn't, right?" Div scowled. "Because I've given up on the Force, I can't even be trusted to recognize my own brother. Not like *you* can. Even if you barely knew him. Only cared enough to leave him to die."

Ferus flinched. Div cursed himself for doing it again: striking Ferus exactly where it was guaranteed to hurt the most.

"Just be careful," Ferus said without resentment. "Don't let your guard down. Don't think you can trust him."

"I don't trust anyone," Div said.

Just another thing he and X-7 had in common.

Before Ferus could reply, Luke, Leia, and Han burst into the shack. "We got them!" Luke said triumphantly, waving a memory chip in the air.

Han arched an eyebrow. *"We?"*

Luke rolled his eyes. "Okay. *Han* got the blueprints."

"And then *we* got Han out before the Imperials turned him into a scorch mark," Leia put in. "And by the way, you're welcome."

"And *you're* delusional," Han said. "If I hadn't been around to save both of your scrawny necks, you'd be dianoga food by now."

Ferus cleared his throat. At once, they fell silent. Div marveled at the way Ferus somehow commanded their respect despite that no one knew who he really was. Even Leia, who always acted like he was worthless, followed his lead. Not for the first time, Div wondered why Ferus had kept close to her all those years, pretending to be someone he wasn't. Ferus refused to speak of it.

This wasn't unusual. Ferus spoke little and often fell into long, heavy silences, staring into nothingness. He was just as kind and determined as ever, but some piece of him was gone.

"It sounds like X-7 is ready, too," Ferus said.

Luke shook his head, a fierce scowl crossing his face. "We have the blueprints; we don't need *him*."

"We can use him," Div countered.

"How are we supposed to use him when we can't trust him?" Luke asked.

"You have another plan?" Ferus said.

Luke and Han glanced at each other, and Han gave

a small nod. "We've been working on something," Luke said, pulling up the blueprints on his datapad. "If we go in through the south entrance . . ." He traced his index finger along the route.

There was a hint of movement in the shadows. A rustling, as soft as a whisper. Div looked up, on alert, but saw nothing.

As the others hunched over the datapad, Ferus caught his eye. He gave Div a nearly imperceptible nod.

So Ferus had heard it, too.

Div kept his head down, but his eyes flicked from side to side as he sought out their intruder. There was no further noise or movement, but Div could feel his presence.

How long had he been there?

And how much had he heard?

Div half listened as Luke and Han laid out their plan. His mind raced furiously, searching for a way to spin this to his advantage. And by the time the planning ended and the others slipped out, he was ready.

The last to go, Ferus hesitated on his way out. "Do you need me to—"

"Go," Div said firmly. Ferus didn't argue. He just tapped his hip, where Div could see the faint outline of a lightsaber hidden beneath his coat. Then he pointed at Div and left without another word. He didn't need words; his meaning was clear.

May the Force be with you.

Div waited in the dark. *May the Force be with me,* he thought wryly. *I'd rather you left me with your lightsaber.*

He had his blaster, of course. But he had a feeling that this time the blaster might not be enough.

Long minutes passed. Nothing happened. "You can come out now," he said loudly. "I'm not leaving until you do."

X-7 emerged from the shadows. He held his blaster in a trembling hand. "I should have known," he said.

"You did know," Div said, forcing himself to remain calm. If X-7 had overheard the conversation with Ferus, then all was lost. But there'd been no sign of his presence then. If all he'd overheard was the Rebels discussing their mission, then things could still be salvaged. Maybe. "That's why you followed me here. You wanted it to be true. You *wanted* me to be working with the Rebels."

"And you let me listen," X-7 said. "You wouldn't have done that unless . . ."

"That's right," Div said, encouraging him. "Unless I *wanted* you there. This isn't just any Rebel mission; this is the Imperial garrison built on the site of the first Imperial munitions factory. The one that—" He swallowed hard. He wouldn't need to fake the emotion. It flooded back whenever he thought about that day. "I've been waiting a long time for this opportunity, to show the Empire that they can't just destroy my family, my planet, without consequences. This is payback."

"Revenge," X-7 said in a dreamy voice.

Div realized that he had finally hit on a human emotion that X-7 understood. "Revenge," he agreed. "For what the Empire did to Clive and Astri — and to you. I've always known this moment would come. But I thought when it did, I would be alone."

X-7 lowered the blaster. He crossed the room in three long, swift strides and clasped Div's hand, then squeezed. "You won't," he said. Abruptly, he dropped his hand, and his tone turned businesslike. "Tell your Rebel friends I have all the Imperial access codes they need. I can obtain the necessary security clearances. Anything you need. We will have our revenge."

It was all working out better than Div could ever have hoped — assuming X-7 was telling the truth.

Revenge.

It was the thought that got him through the day, and the next. It was the dream. Revenge on the people who had slaughtered his family, who had stolen his identity. It was the only thing about this new life that made sense. By day, Div showed him holopic after holopic, strangers' faces that meant nothing to him, memories of another life, belonging to another man. And when the stars came out, so did the nightmares. More strangers, calling out for him. Green grass and sparkling seas and a feeling, alien and unwelcome. *Happy.* He woke every morning in a cold sweat, and only one thing calmed him down. One word.

Revenge.

This was the act that would unite his past and present. It would restore sanity to his insane world. He was Trever Flume, a passionate warrior; he was X-7, a heartless assassin. Two identities, galaxies apart, united by a single need.

Revenge.

Whatever he was, whatever he had been, he was a killer. He would kill, he would destroy, he would avenge. X-7 would repay his debt to Trever Flume, to the name, the body he wore like a costume. He would join the Rebels. He would help them tear down the walls of the Imperial garrison. His true nature would emerge in the hot crucible of revenge. Either he would strip away the years of X-7 and embrace Trever Flume, or Trever would die — really die this time — in the fire that incinerated the garrison, and X-7 would be free.

Finally, things had started making sense again. And then, the day before the attack, they stopped.

Alone in the strange house, he sat stiffly in a hard-backed chair. It was the only place he felt comfortable. This house, it was a place of comfort, of *decadence*. With its plush overstuffed couches, its fully stocked kitchen, its luxuriously soft mattresses and picture windows, it wasn't a house for a man like him, a man of discipline. A man of action.

He had come downstairs planning to look at more pictures, dull as they were with their endless grinning faces. Strangers — now nothing but corpses — who meant nothing to him.

But he couldn't face them.

I have to leave this place, he thought, standing abruptly. Suddenly certain. *Now, forever.*

But he didn't move. Because it was just as certain that he had to stay. There was Div. There was his empty past. There was *revenge.*

This place was tearing him apart.

He was standing there, frozen and undecided, when his comlink pinged with an incoming message. And everything fell apart.

Don't believe the lies, the message said. Transmitted on an encrypted channel. *If you want the truth, all you need do is ask.* There was no name, but there was a time. And an address.

X-7 knew it was likely a trap. But what kind of trap could contain him?

Only a trap of lies, he thought. He told himself that no one had the ability to lie to him; he was too good at seeing through pathetic human deception. Except that was no longer true, was it? Emotions clouded everything, dulling the sharp edges of the world. It was possible Div was lying to him and he was just too foolish to see it. If there was more truth to be found, he had to have it.

And if someone was trying to trap him, X-7 had to know who it was. You had to know your enemy before you could kill it.

The building was empty, but it didn't look abandoned.

There was no thick layer of dust, no broken trans-paristeel, no apparent garbage or squatters, nothing to indicate that the building had been deserted for more than a few days, if that. It was a stout, unassuming building tucked into a cluster of faceless high-rises. The Imperial presence in this city was unusually heavy. Stormtroopers were posted at regular intervals, noting the movements of the citizens. X-7 knew that the Rebels believed that destroying the garrison would be the first step in reclaiming Belazura. They hoped the city would rebel against its Imperial rulers and rediscover the courage that had let them battle the Empire for so long. But X-7 had his doubts. The faces he passed weren't the faces of Rebels. They were the faces of defeated, terrified cowards who'd learned their lessons about fighting back. Astri Divinian and Clive Flax hadn't been the only ones to die that day ten years earlier. The day the weapons factory was destroyed, the city had rebelled. Three thousand Belazurans had been killed.

Those who had survived weren't eager to be punished again.

Before going in, X-7 made a thorough survey of the perimeter. His modified infrared goggles let him peer through the walls and search for heat signatures, telltale signs of an enemy lying in wait. But he saw nothing. He drew his blaster and stepped inside.

It was only one room, large and echoing, lit by nothing but the dim glow of the setting suns, filtering through dirty transparisteel. Ten meters by ten meters, ample windows and doors to serve as escape routes. Which, of course, meant ample points for possible attack. He prowled the edge of the wide room, turning in slow circles with his weapon raised. No surprises this time, no one sneaking up on him from behind. It would be easier if he knew what he was searching for. A person? A message?

A bomb?

There was a soft, nearly inaudible click. X-7 went on high alert, spinning wildly, searching in vain for the source of the noise. The building was still empty. Then the silence was broken by a whirring hum, machinery springing into motion. Certain of only one thing — the need to *leave* — X-7 pivoted and raced toward the nearest exit.

A durasteel shutter slammed down across the door, blocking his way.

The room echoed with the clang of durasteel on duracrete as the thick, heavy shutters slammed down all around him, covering every window, every door, every means of escape. All except for one: The entrance to a turbolift had suddenly appeared in a previously blank wall of duracrete.

X-7 combed the room, centimeter by centimeter, making sure there wasn't any other option. There wasn't. So he stepped into the turbolift.

As soon as the doors slid shut, the bottom dropped out beneath him. The lift zoomed downward, then abruptly stopped and whooshed horizontally for several long seconds. X-7 calculated that he was at least twenty meters below the ground, traveling two, possibly three city blocks. He'd come across such contraptions on other planets, underground turbolifts, buildings connected by secret passageways. The Rebels were like borrats, hollowing out warrens in the heart of every city so they could operate beneath the Imperial radar. But X-7 was certain no Rebel cells were operating on Belazura — none, that is, except for the one he'd found himself a part of.

Without warning, the turbolift started to rise.

As it came to a stop, X-7 gauged the speed and the time and, with a simple calculation, judged himself to be about twenty stories off the ground. Too high to jump, if it came to that. But not too high to climb.

The doors soundlessly slid open, revealing an office nearly identical to one he'd recently visited on Coruscant. Its occupant stood behind the imposing desk, clearly waiting for X-7's arrival.

X-7's first reaction was relief. His body wanted to drop to its knees, beg forgiveness from his commander.

"Surprised?" Rezi Soresh raised his eyebrows. "But not disappointed, I hope?"

X-7 raised his blaster and pulled the trigger.

CHAPTER
THIRTEEN

The shot tore into the wall behind Soresh's head.

Soresh sighed. "This is Sittana marble and it certainly looks better without holes in it," he said. "But I suppose I should thank you for not putting one in my head."

"What are you doing here?" X-7 asked harshly.

"Oh, your Rebel reconnaissance didn't reveal that I was in the neighborhood?" Soresh asked with false shock. X-7 kept his face blank. So Soresh knew about the Rebel plans — which meant they were doomed. "I'm supervising the new munitions shipments — and more to the point, I'm supervising *you*. You think I can afford to have an agent running wild through the galaxy? In *this* condition? That should be obvious. No, the question you should be asking is why are *you* here?" He formed a temple with his fingers and propped his chin on his fingertips. "I didn't train you to be the kind of man who could be surprised."

He pressed something on his desk, and the door to the turbolift disappeared into the wall. A bookshelf took its place. X-7 cursed himself for letting his one guaranteed means of exit disappear.

"Old Rebel hideaway," Soresh said, gesturing at the hidden turbolift, obviously pleased with himself. "Of course, there aren't any of them left to hide. We took care of that."

X-7 did his best to ignore Soresh. Automatically, he surveyed his surroundings, eyes alighting on any possible means of escape. The office, clearly a temporary one, was mostly bare, although the Commander had stupidly left his files and datapad sitting out on the desk. Perhaps he'd forgotten that he'd equipped X-7 with a photographic memory. Once the information passed in front of his face, it was in his mind forever. The desk also contained the controls for the hidden turbolift. Once the Commander was out of commission — which would be easy enough to see to — the lift would be accessible.

And if all else failed, there was always the window.

Soresh waved a hand lazily at the transparisteel. "Go," he said. "If that's what you really want. I didn't think you were the kind of man who would enjoy living a lie, but be my guest."

"There are only two things I want," X-7 retorted. "My life — and your death." He watched his commander carefully, searching for some sign of anxiety or concern. But the man remained perfectly calm. Confident. *What does he know that I don't?* X-7 thought, suddenly wary. Maybe he should leave sooner rather than later.

But if he left, the Commander would always be waiting to reassert control, to turn X-7 back into a slave. It would be much more expedient to kill him now.

Think like a human, X-7 reminded himself. *Let yourself feel.*

Fine, then. Not just *expedient.* It would be satisfying — it would be *just* — to watch the Commander die.

Soresh burst into laughter. "*Want?* You don't know the meaning of the word."

"You know nothing about me," X-7 said. "Not anymore."

"I know *everything* about you." Soresh's voice was like a dragonsnake, slithering into X-7's ears, into his brain. Laced with venom. "Certainly more than you know about yourself."

"And I know about *you,*" X-7 spat out. "Your precious program, your *volunteers.* We were *prisoners.* You told me I'd enlisted, that all I wanted was to serve the Empire. I was a *Rebel.* You killed me, the real me — you made me a murderer and turned me against my own."

"Whining doesn't become you," the Commander

said. But his voice had tightened, nearly imperceptibly. His eyelids fluttered. X-7 knew the signs. He'd hit a nerve. "Nor does stupidity. You actually believe their lies?"

"I can see when a man is telling the truth," X-7 said coolly. "You taught me well."

"Fine." The Commander stood. "You weren't a volunteer. None of you were. But you're not this, this pathetic *Trever Flume* they're trying to turn you into, either. It's a trap. Don't be such a fool that you walk right into it."

X-7 scanned the Commander's face for evidence that this, too, was a lie. But he could find none.

It doesn't mean anything, he thought. The Commander was a practiced manipulator.

And X-7 wasn't exactly objective when it came to listening to his lies.

"I don't believe you," he said steadily. He wouldn't let Soresh sense *his* inner hesitation. Perhaps he was becoming more human, more *Trever,* but enough of him was still X-7. His thoughts, his doubts remained his own.

"Believe me; don't believe me. That's irrelevant. Haven't you figured it out yet?" The Commander twisted his face into a gruesome smile. "It doesn't *matter* who you were. *Trever Flume,* or some other fool, whoever it was, that man is dead. There's no going backward, no hiding in the past. No becoming *ordinary* again. Why would you ever want such a thing? You're better than that. Stronger, faster, smarter. Harder. Better because *I* made you that way. You think you can make yourself soft again? Make yourself stupid? Please. You're a weapon, razor sharp. Be grateful."

"To *you*?" X-7 whispered harshly, and drew out a slim vibroblade. The blaster would be quicker, surer. But he wanted satisfaction.

"You can thank me later," Soresh said breezily. "Or kill me now, if that's what you really *want*. If you hate your creator so very much. Kill me."

It was all the invitation X-7 needed. He raised the blade. Stepped forward.

Tried to step forward. But it was like his shoes were nailed to the floor.

"Problem?" The Commander smiled. "Let me help you out." He took a step toward X-7. Then another, and another, until they were standing face to face.

Now, X-7 thought. But his limbs were frozen. And his mind was screaming in pain.

He hadn't had any trouble holding the blade to the Commander's throat before. But that had been different. Then he had only intended to scare Soresh. Now, with murder running through his veins, he couldn't move. Could barely breathe.

"Feeling out of sorts?" Soresh said smugly. "Limbs a little heavy? Chest a little constricted?"

X-7 tried to speak, but found he couldn't even do that. The more desperately he wanted to kill the Commander, the more rigid and useless his limbs became. It was becoming an effort to stand. The vibroblade was heavy and awkward in his numb fingers. Distantly, he felt it drop to the floor.

And the pain . . .

X-7 had suffered pain before. He had been bred for pain. But this was different. It had no source; it came from within.

"You can't hurt me," the Commander said, "because I'm your master, whether you choose to forget that or not. Your *mind* will never forget. Your *programming* will never forget." He clapped a hand on X-7's shoulder. X-7 spat in his face. The Commander didn't even bother to wipe it off. "Let this be a lesson to you," he said, saliva dripping down his cheek. "*Humans* have free will. But you have only *my* will. You're not a person anymore. You're a tool. You're a program. You are, and will always be, *mine.*"

X-7 finally understood.

Take me home. The words formed themselves in his brain, almost without his intention. But he knew that if he were to try to form them, his mouth would comply. He would be able to move. His rebellious body would fall into line again, ready to serve the Commander. It would be easy. He opened his mouth.

And the window exploded.

CHAPTER FOURTEEN

Luke burst through the window, Div and Han close behind him. X-7 was standing face to face with an Imperial officer, both of them as still as stone. "Come on!" Luke shouted. X-7 didn't move; he didn't even turn in the direction of the commotion. The Imperial blanched at the sight of the Rebels and their blasters. He backed away, stumbling over his own feet, and ducked beneath his desk. One hand groped blindly on the desk, feeling around for the comlink. "Security!" he shouted in a high, fluttery voice. "Emergency! Security!"

"X-7, come on," Luke said urgently.

"Enough," Han said. He grabbed X-7 and slipped a hook at the end of the liquid-cable line around X-7's belt buckle. "Let's get out of here while we still can." He gave the liquid cable a harsh yank. X-7 started, as if suddenly realizing they were there.

"What . . . ?"

But there was no time. The Rebels dragged X-7 toward the window. As one, they jumped.

It was heart-stopping, flying into midair like that, the ground so many stories beneath. But the cable caught. "All clear?" Div said into the comlink.

"All clear," Leia's voice reported.

Luke nodded. "Coming up." He pressed the retraction switch, and the line went taut, then yanked him up the side of the building. Div, Han, and X-7 dangled a few meters beneath him.

It would be easy for Luke to reach across with his lightsaber and sever X-7's line. It wouldn't even be that difficult to make it look like an accident. X-7 would plummet to the ground, and Luke would never have to look into his cold eyes again. He would never have to pretend they were allies.

And he wouldn't have to force himself to *trust* X-7 — to once again put his life in the traitor's hands.

But the edge of the roof was drawing nearer and nearer. Ferus's arm dangled over the side. He gripped Luke's arm and hauled him onto the roof. The moment was gone.

We should have just left him, Luke thought.

But this rescue mission wasn't about helping X-7. It was about protecting a valuable resource, their newest weapon against the Empire. Nothing could be more important than that.

• • •

"We should call it off," Luke argued. "Bad enough that the Empire knows Rebels are on Belazura —"

"Because *you* screwed up the blueprint retrieval," Div pointed out angrily.

Luke ignored him. They might be in Div's house, but it was Leia's mission. She was the one he had to convince. "If X-7 compromised us with the Imperials —"

"We are *not* calling it off," Div snapped. "After everything we've done? General Rieekan gave me his word."

"Nobody wants this," Leia said. "But we have to proceed carefully."

"I say we proceed right off this rock," Han said. "Now, before the Empire comes calling."

Leia scowled. "Of course *you* want to run."

"It's not about running," Han argued. "It's about being *smart*."

"And what would you know about that?" Leia asked.

Han leaned forward, jabbing a finger at the princess. "Listen to me, Your Worshipfulness. *You* face down a mean Klatooinian, a crazy Ortolan, and a Chiss with an anger-management problem and a CryoBan grenade — all on the same night. And *then* you talk to me about running away. I'd like to see *you* try to tie a Klatooinian to the back of a wild rancor."

"And I'd like to see *you* swallowed up by a —"

"I may have a solution."

Everyone looked up. X-7 had appeared in the room with his usual silent stealth. He'd spoken only once since they'd fled Soresh's roof in a stolen airspeeder. And that wasn't to say thank you. It was only to ask how they'd known where he was — and why they were following him. "I lost you once," Div had said, thinking quickly. "I wasn't about to lose you again." Accepting that, X-7 had fallen into a stony silence. Until now.

"Since it's my fault that you're in this position," X-7 continued, "your having felt the need to . . . *rescue* me."

There was something off about the way he said the word, Luke thought. *Rescue.* As if it was an insult. But his face was placid, his voice pleasant; nothing to indicate that he was anything less than sincere. Nothing but Luke's vague misgivings.

"While I was a guest of Commander Soresh, I had a chance to learn a few things," X-7 said, keeping his eyes on Div. "One of particular interest to you, I believe. Tomorrow, at sixteen hundred hours, an Imperial delegation will be arriving on Belazura for a tour of the Imperial garrison. A delegation that includes Darth Vader."

It was as if all the air had been sucked out of the room.

"Vader?" Luke repeated. *"Here?"*

X-7 nodded.

Leia's face had gone pale. Luke knew she held Darth Vader responsible for the destruction of Alderaan. Responsible for the deaths of everyone she loved.

And it was Vader's lightsaber that had struck Ben to the ground.

Vader was the evil engine at the heart of the Empire, doing the Emperor's dark bidding. He was an enforcer, a last resort, the ultimate threat. And without him, the Empire might well begin to crumble.

This could be it. The beginning of the end. *If* they could pull off the attack. If X-7's intel could be trusted.

"We go forward," Leia said in a commanding tone. "Tomorrow, Belazura's Imperial garrison goes up in smoke."

Luke nodded, trying to suppress his doubts. "And Vader with it."

I t was time.

The Rebels gathered in the small Divinian compound. They inventoried their weapons, made one last survey of the garrison blueprints, rehearsed the plan one final time. And then they set out to destroy the Empire's seat of power on Belazura.

Or die trying.

X-7 suppressed a smile. He knew which it would be. He was just sorry he wouldn't be around to watch. "Div, wait," he said, pulling his so-called brother away from the others. "I need to talk to you for a minute. In private."

Div looked indecisively back and forth between X-7 and the departing Rebels. "Can it wait?"

"It really can't," X-7 said. "Brother."

Div checked the time on his datapad and nodded. "Five minutes," he agreed. "Then we need to get into position."

X-7 didn't say anything.

"Well?" Div asked. "What is it?"

"Not here." X-7 led him upstairs, into the room that had once belonged to Trever. He shut the door.

He had considered letting Div go, showing some form of mercy to the man who might be his adopted brother. But that impulse was just a symptom of the sickness, the rot that had eaten away at his insides, turning his durasteel will to Sarkanian jelly. And Div was at the root of it all. These memories, these delusions, these repulsive *feelings,* they all revolved around Div and his stories of the past. He was the only link to Trever, the only thing tethering X-7 to humanity. With Div gone, Trever would die forever.

X-7 would be free.

"What's going on?" Div asked. X-7 could tell he was starting to get suspicious.

He should just *do* it. But he wasn't ready. Not yet.

"I couldn't let you go with them," he said. He turned his back to Div, picked up one of the old photo albums, and leafed through. Shot after shot of Trever and Lune, happy boys, happy together. But he wasn't looking at the images. The photo album shielded him as he drew the palm-sized laser blaster from his coat, readied himself to fire. At point-blank range, there would be no risk of error.

"What? Why not?"

"They're all going to die," X-7 said coldly. "The Empire is waiting for them to arrive. As you should have been waiting for me." He whirled around, raised the blaster.

But he didn't pull the trigger.

Div froze. His eyes widened. "You sent them into an ambush?" he said.

"You're worried about your friends?" X-7 asked. *"Now?"*

It was the final straw. If *this* was what it meant to be human, X-7 wanted nothing to do with it. Ignoring the threat to one's own life because someone else was in danger? It was the quickest way to die. Other people were like anchors, dragging you down. If you let yourself become attached, you'd inevitably be pulled under.

This, X-7 finally understood, was what made him superior. He'd deceived himself long enough, pretending he could be one of them. He'd torn himself apart, pretending to be someone he wasn't. Pretending to be *someone.*

It was a lie. He was no one.

He was X-7.

There was no escaping that.

"What is this?" Div said quickly. "We've been over and over this. It's not a trap. Everything I've told you has been the absolute truth. You're my —"

"Brother," X-7 said. "Don't worry. I believe you."

Div released a nearly imperceptible sigh.

"That's why I need to do this," X-7 said.

He fired.

"Something's wrong," Luke whispered, nervously adjusting his maintenance uniform as they approached the garrison's workers' entrance.

"Of course something's wrong," Han shot back, sounding annoyed. "We're walking into an Imperial garrison. Two of us against two hundred of them. And we're doing it voluntarily. What's *not* wrong about that?" He hoisted his toolbox, which held six Merr-Sonn Munitions Class-A thermal detonators. The plan was simple. They would use the security access codes X-7 had given them. Div and X-7 were doing the same on the opposite end of the garrison. They would sneak in, place the detonators at the heart of the building, a weapons arsenal, where any explosion would ignite a wider blaze. The detonators were on a timer set for thirty minutes. Just as Darth Vader was surveying his latest triumph, the building would explode.

Two Rebel strike forces under Leia's command were positioned around the perimeter of the building, ready to go at a moment's notice.

Han reached the designated entrance. He raised his hand to enter the code that would let them slip in unnoticed. Without thinking, Luke grabbed his wrist to stop him.

"What now, kid?" Han asked irritably. "If you don't have the stomach for this —"

"It's not that," Luke whispered. "Something's wrong."

He had that feeling, the dark, suffocating cloud that sometimes descended over him when danger was near. The Force, warning him of trouble. But it wasn't just that. It was something he *didn't* feel — something missing.

The last time he'd been near Darth Vader, he'd sensed a different darkness. He hadn't understood it then, but he remembered it vividly. It was *power*, sizzling in the air, like the change in air pressure before a storm, subtle at first, then overwhelming.

And it was missing.

"Vader isn't here," Luke said.

"How would you know?" Han asked.

"I just know." And if X-7 had been lying about Vader's presence, what else had he been lying about?

Han shook his head. Luke knew he had little patience for what he thought of as Jedi mumbo jumbo, which meant Luke wasn't going to convince him with talk of gut feelings and trusting the Force. He had to speak in a language Han understood.

"You don't trust X-7 any more than I do," Luke pointed out.

Han didn't disagree.

Luke pushed on. "So if he gave us the wrong codes —"

"Kid, if X-7's against us, we've got bigger problems than the wrong codes," Han said. "And —" He jerked his head toward the AC-1 surveillance droids keeping their mechanical eyes on the entrance. "It's probably already too late." He gave the barrel of his blaster a loving tap. "But it's not like we're going in unprepared."

"Two of us and two hundred of them," Luke reminded him. "You're prepared for *that*?"

Han laughed. He entered the security code. The door slid open. No stormtroopers, no alarms, no nothing. "Looks like you were worried about nothing," Han said as they stepped inside.

Then his comlink pinged. "Luke! Han!" Leia's tinny voice blared through the static. "It's a trap —" Her voice was cut off by the thunder of an explosion.

The transmission went dead.

Ferus didn't know why he'd been compelled to turn back. To anyone else — to Leia, especially — it would look cowardly. He'd abandoned his designated post for no particular reason. He'd fled the base just before the Rebel raid was to begin, and was headed as fast as he could to the relative safety of the Divinian compound. It was irrational and unexpected. But it wasn't cowardice.

It was a certainty that something was very wrong.

And the ghost of a voice, whispering in his ears.

Go.

It could have been Obi-Wan's voice, speaking from beyond the grave. But Ferus believed it was his own. And he followed it.

The Divinian house was empty. Ferus prowled the rooms one by one, lightsaber at the ready. There was something off here. He could sense it. He flung open door after door. Kitchen. Refresher. Bedroom. A second bedroom —

Ferus gasped and rushed across the room. "Div!" he shouted, kneeling by the body.

The boy's eyes were closed. A blast of laserfire had scorched his shoulder. Ferus pressed two fingers to Div's pale neck. He closed his eyes. "Please," he whispered, feeling for a pulse.

It was there. Faint, but there. He was alive.

"Come on," Ferus urged him, hurriedly dressing the wound. "Stay with me. Stay with me, Lune."

"How many times do I have to tell you that's not my name?" Div opened his eyes and gave Ferus a weak smile.

"What happened?"

Div struggled to sit up.

"Easy," Ferus said. "Go slow."

Div shook his head. "No time. Head for the garrison. It's an ambush."

"X-7?"

"I don't know what happened. He just . . . turned."

"He shot you in the shoulder," Ferus mused, tucking Div's left arm into a makeshift sling.

"I noticed."

"Interesting."

Div dragged himself to his feet, wincing at the pain. "You find this *interesting*?"

"He is a trained Imperial assassin, and he shot you point-blank — in the shoulder," Ferus said, helping Div stand. "If he'd wanted you dead, you'd be dead. Makes you wonder."

"Makes *you* wonder, maybe," Div said. "Makes me want to go save our friends from walking into a bloodbath."

Div was pale and trembling with the effort of standing. The sling kept his shoulder immobile, but moving was clearly agony. "I'm not sure how much help you can be to anyone in this condition," Ferus said, worried.

Div just stared at him with the same determined, unsettling gaze he'd had as a child. "I have to try."

"Go!" Luke urged Han. "I'll plant the detonators. You help Leia."

Han was already in motion. The Rebel strike forces had camouflaged themselves in the wooded hills surrounding the garrison. Now their hiding place was lit up by exploding grenades and bolts of laserfire crackling through the trees. It had been an ambush, and the Rebel forces were surely overpowered. There was no chance that Han's presence would turn the tide, even with the fragmentation grenades tucked into his belt beside his backup blaster. If he was smart, he'd just walk away, save his own skin while he had the chance. But he didn't hesitate to plunge into the smoky battle.

Chewbacca was in there somewhere.

Leia was in there.

It was total chaos. Laserfire shot through the thick haze of smoke. The nahtival trees were on fire. The branches crackled as they burned, and flaming leaves fluttered through the air, igniting small patches of zura-grass. The Rebels and the stormtroopers seemed to be firing blindly, desperate to hit someone — anyone.

There were at least twice as many stormtroopers as there were Rebels. Han bashed the nearest one in the back of the head and pushed forward into the center of the mess.

Laserfire peppered the trees. "Chewie!" Han shouted, catching sight of the Wookiee surrounded by four stormtroopers. Chewbacca grabbed one in each hand and swung them like a stun baton into the others. The Imperials went down in a grunting heap.

"Get down, buddy!" Han shouted as a stormtrooper perched in a tree began shooting at the Wookiee. Han whipped his blaster into action and took him out with a single shot to the head. The Imperial toppled to the ground, landing with a clatter on two of his allies.

Chewbacca roared in gratitude, already turning toward a couple of Rebels pinned down by a circle of troopers. Han was charging in to help when a blast of laserfire shot past, singeing his shoulder. He flinched, whipping around to return fire. But his assailant was already down. Leia stood over the body. She snatched the trooper's fallen blaster rifle and tossed it to Han.

"Behind you!" she cried.

Han snatched the rifle out of the air as he spun

around, now firing with both hands at the approaching stormtroopers. Three toppled over. But another burst of laserfire pelted his leg. He staggered, trying to ignore the pain.

"Took you long enough," Leia said with false cheer. She and Han positioned themselves back to back, spraying laserfire at any Imperials who came too close. Bodies in white armor littered the ground, but they lay side by side with fallen Rebels. Too many of them. "Where's Luke?"

"He went in," Han said.

"You let him go alone?" Leia shouted. She blasted a stormtrooper, but from the tone of her voice, Han suspected she had another target in mind.

"Excuse me if I thought you could use a little *help* here," Han growled as the air split with the roaring engine of an approaching Imperial airspeeder. Han lobbed one of his fragmentation grenades, and the speeder exploded in midair, showering the battle with fiery shards of durasteel.

"We should go help him," Leia said.

"After you," Han drawled, gesturing toward the circle of stormtroopers surrounding them. It seemed that the more they felled, the more reinforcements appeared. It was impossible: no escape, no retreat, and no helping Luke. "Don't worry, the kid can handle himself."

"I hope you're right," Leia said.

I'd better be, Han thought. An explosion in the heart

of the garrison might just send the stormtroopers into a panicked retreat.

Otherwise . . . well, he had two blasters, six rounds of ammunition, an angry Wookiee, and an even angrier princess on his side. He just hoped it would be enough.

Luke strode down a corridor filled with Imperial officers, keeping his eyes straight ahead and trying to pretend he belonged. They barely glanced at him, their eyes noting his maintenance uniform, then skimming over him as if he was an inanimate object. He couldn't understand why his presence hadn't raised an alarm. Was it possible that X-7 hadn't betrayed them? That something else had revealed the Rebel presence to the Empire?

Possible, maybe, but Luke didn't buy it. Something else was going on here.

But while he tried to figure out what, he made his way as casually as possible to the primary arsenal hold, where the majority of the weapons were stored. He still had the thermal detonators; he still had a mission. His friends were counting on him to complete it. Belazura was counting on him.

He had memorized the blueprints. The garrison was a mazelike fortress, its twisting passageways turning in on themselves and dead-ending without warning. It had been designed to confuse its occupants, even the ones with top secret clearance — because there was always something even *more* top secret. The Empire thrived on secrecy, even the highest officers operating in ignorance of the Emperor's true plans. The garrison had been designed with that philosophy in mind. As Luke wound his way deeper and deeper into the heart of the building, he began to wonder if he'd ever make it out.

X-7's security codes ushered him through checkpoint after checkpoint. Luke remained certain he was walking into a trap, but there was nothing to do but keep going. He reached the access point to the weapons arsenal. Two stormtroopers manned the door. "Authorized personnel only," one of them informed him.

"I am authorized," Luke said, offering the security card that had helped him through the other checkpoints. He noted the security pad over the door. It wasn't a keypad, like the others he'd seen. This one required a handprint.

The guards didn't move to let him pass. "You don't have clearance."

Pulling out a blaster would only alarm them. But the hilt of his deactivated lightsaber looked like an innocent piece of durasteel. Harmless. He gripped it, ready.

"No one enters without level-four clearance," the stormtrooper said. "No maintenance."

"But I have —"

"This is TBR-312," the stormtrooper said into his comlink. "Unauthorized personnel —"

Luke flung his arm out, activating the lightsaber as it swung toward the stormtrooper. The comlink dropped from his hand. His counterpart swiveled a blaster toward Luke. But Luke was already diving for the floor. He somersaulted toward the first stormtrooper, slashing with a smoother, upward jab, just as Div had taught him. It sliced through the white plastoid armor, and the stormtrooper dropped.

Luke leapt immediately back to his feet and jumped away from the other trooper's blasts. He struggled to get close enough to land a blow, but the laserfire kept him on the defensive.

Remember what Div taught you, he thought.

Luke spun and leapt into the air, slashing the beam with a diagonal thrust. The stormtrooper stumbled backward, firing blindly. Luke intercepted the beam, angling the blade to deflect the bolt back at the stormtrooper. It slammed into his chest, knocking him to the ground. He clutched once at his scorched armor and then was still.

Luke removed the stormtrooper's glove and pressed the trooper's hand to the palm-recognition security interface. The door slid open, revealing a massive chamber at least fifty meters wide and three stories high. Laser cannons, heavy turbolasers, and concussion missiles were stockpiled everywhere. As the Rebels had guessed, this was the perfect spot. Luke dragged the stormtroopers' bodies into the room and shut the door again. Then he fumbled with the toolbox, pulling out the detonators.

The Imperial comlink crackled to life. "Report, TBR-312. What is the situation?"

"No situation," Luke said quickly into the comlink. "Everything is under control."

It wouldn't hold them off for long. He began planting the detonators, carefully choosing the largest of the weapons stockpiles. He worked quickly, setting the timer for fifteen minutes rather than the planned thirty. It would give him less time to escape — but better to be caught in the blast than give the Imperials enough time to discover and defuse the charges.

Maybe it was inevitable that the Imperials would catch him. But by the time they did, it would be too late.

X-7 stalked his prey like a manka cat. Stealthy and silent as a shadow, he trailed Luke Skywalker, waiting for his moment.

Div was dead. Up in the hills, the Rebel forces were, even now, being slaughtered like a herd of banthas. And now just a single loose end remained — one mission that belonged to him alone. Skywalker was the first target who had avoided his attack. That had been the beginning of all this. The failure to kill Skywalker had put X-7 on a collision path with his disgusting human emotions, his disgusting human past. And since Skywalker had been the beginning, he would also be the end.

X-7 hadn't tipped the Empire off to the Rebels' entire plan. He'd given them the coordinates of the hidden Rebels. But he'd led them away from Skywalker. This kill was his.

As slow and clumsy as he was, the Rebel had managed to make his way into the arsenal. The giant chamber stored hundreds of weapons: mines, ion cannons, turbolasers — everything the Empire could ever need to subdue a planet. If any of the Rebels had had brains in their heads, they would have realized that *stealing* the weapons would be far more efficient than *destroying* them. But of course, the Rebels never thought; they just acted. It was why they were doomed to lose. Luke was determined to destroy the garrison and the weapons it housed — and he'd chosen exactly the right spot. Even a small explosion would touch off an inferno. It would be enough firepower to take down the entire building. Perfect for Skywalker's purposes.

It would also be enough noise — massive load-lifter droids restocking the weaponry — to cover X-7's footsteps as he crept along the catwalk far overhead.

Perfect for X-7's purposes.

X-7 readied his laser rifle. Took aim. *No one to save you this time,* he thought, watching Luke's tiny figure through the scope. *This time, you die.*

X-7's finger twitched toward the trigger.

Div launched himself at X-7, knocking him off balance. They tumbled to the ground. X-7's blast rifle flew out of his hand. He slammed a fist into Div's shoulder, jabbing it squarely into Div's wound. Div clenched his teeth, trying to ignore the pain, but his shoulder spasmed. X-7 hit the wound again, harder, and shoved him aside. Div struggled to fight back, but his strength was failing.

And then a glowing blade slashed down. X-7 threw himself out of the way just in time. Ferus struck again.

"I know what you are," X-7 gasped, springing to his feet and moving out of the way of the beam. "I've always known. You don't scare me, Jedi."

Ferus advanced, lightsaber raised. "I should."

Furious at his weakness, Div could do nothing but watch the fierce battle play out. Far below them, Luke had already finished setting the thermal detonators. *Escape while you still can,* Div urged him silently. But even if Div had shouted it, Luke never would have heard him over the thunder of the machinery.

Ferus slashed at X-7 with the blue blade. X-7 jumped-sidestepped out of the way, and suddenly, the assassin produced a lightwhip, crackling with deadly laser energy. He flicked it at Ferus, who leapt over the snakelike rope and somersaulted along the catwalk.

"Not bad, old man," X-7 said. "But not good enough." Swinging the whip in a deadly arc with one hand, he wielded a blaster with the other. The weapon sent a wide spray of laserfire at Ferus, who was trapped against the railing with no cover. He slipped between the bursts of laserfire with nearly impossible speed and agility, then nimbly hopped onto the railing and balanced on the five-centimeter-wide durasteel.

X-7 released an icy chuckle and struck out with the whip, trying to knock Ferus off his perch. But Ferus used the height to his advantage, his lightsaber bearing down on X-7's arm. X-7 stifled a cry of pain and dropped the blaster. A bloody stain spread across his shirt. He went into a frenzy, hacking and slashing with his good arm. The whip whistled through the air. It caught Ferus on the leg, only a light blow, but enough to knock him off balance. He toppled backward — and disappeared from sight.

Div gasped.

X-7 laughed again. It was a hard, inhuman noise, like grinding gears. He leaned over the railing. Div didn't want to imagine what X-7 saw below. Ferus's broken body, smashed on the duracrete.

"Where are you, old man?" X-7 sounded surprised.

He turned around — just in time to see Ferus spring over the opposite edge of the catwalk, his lightsaber pointed straight at X-7's heart.

His aim was true.

X-7 dropped to the ground, his eyes glassy, his body limp. Blood pooled beneath him. He gasped, as if he couldn't draw enough air. But then his rasping grew louder. He was trying to speak. It was just two syllables, soft but clear.

"Div. Please."

Div looked at Ferus, who offered no guidance. So against his better judgment, Div approached the fallen assassin. He knelt by X-7's side. "What is it?"

He hated the man for what he'd done — to the Rebels, to Luke, to himself. But more, he hated what the man represented. To the end, he'd been a tool of the Empire. A ruthless killer who served other ruthless killers. A symbol of the darkness that shadowed Div's life.

It shouldn't have mattered that for a few days, he'd been something else.

"Brother," X-7 gasped.

Div shook his head.

"My brother. Tell me. You are." With a mighty effort, X-7 slid his body up along the wall, until he was in a half-sitting position. Before he could speak again, his body was racked by a spasm of coughing. He leaned over, spit out a mouthful of phlegm and blood. "I need to know," he said in a clearer voice. His chest heaved. "Before I die. Need to know who I was. If I was someone. That I . . ." X-7 trailed off, his eyes fluttering shut. For a moment, Div thought that was it. The end. But then the eyes opened again, wide and rimmed with red. "I mattered to someone. Need to know."

Trever mattered, Div thought fiercely. *He's been dead for ten years, while you lived. You lived and you killed.*

The man deserved to die alone, broken, without comfort. How dare he ask Div for anything? How dare he expect sympathy, *pity* after all he'd done?

And yet . . .

"You mattered to someone," Div said. "You were someone, once." Because that was true. Someone had been born, had a mother, a father, maybe a brother. Someone had been taken by the Empire, had his memories scrubbed away. Turned into a killer. Maybe it wasn't Trever — but it could have been.

And Div wouldn't have wanted Trever to die alone, no matter what he'd done.

He rested a hand on X-7's shoulder. "You mattered. Brother."

The ghost of a smile crossed X-7's face. He closed his eyes. Div's hand stayed where it was, rising and falling with X-7's shallow breaths, until the breaths stopped.

"He's gone," Ferus said softly behind him.

Div had almost forgotten he was there. "Good riddance," Div said harshly. He stood up. "Let's get out of here before this place blows." Luke was gone. They had thirty minutes — if Luke had set the timer as planned. But nothing else had gone as planned. So they fled the building, Ferus's flashing lightsaber cutting down the few Imperials foolish enough to step into their path. Div's wound throbbed with every step, but he ignored the pain.

They ran side by side, their footfalls in sync. But when they finally stopped, a safe distance away from the garrison, Div turned his back before Ferus could speak.

"Div." Ferus reached for him. Div jerked away. "You're angry," Ferus said. "What is it?"

I'm always angry, Div thought. From their perch on a nearby hill, he watched the garrison, waiting for it to burst into flame. Picturing the look on X-7's face just before the life drained from his eyes.

The building exploded. The ground shook. Flames licked the sky.

It's all happening again, Div thought. Watching an explosion from the hills while his brother's body burned. *Not my brother,* he thought. *But someone's.*

"Aren't you angry?" he finally asked without looking at Ferus. "He sent your friends into an ambush. If we hadn't stopped him just now, he would have murdered Luke."

"You're not angry at him," Ferus said with that maddening Jedi certainty. "You're angry at yourself. For being misled?" He narrowed his eyes, then shook his head. "No, I don't think that's it."

"Do you need me here for this conversation?" Div asked irritably. "Seems like you already have all the answers."

Ferus just waited. Div could be a patient man, but he had the feeling that Ferus could wait forever. And while it would be easy enough to turn his back and leave . . . he didn't.

"Yes, I'm angry!" he spat out. "That I let him die thinking he was Trever. That I let myself . . ."

"That you let yourself think he was Trever," Ferus prompted. "Even for just a moment. You let yourself hope. Nothing wrong with that."

"It was a stupid, childish fantasy," Div growled. "Coincidences like that only happen in storybooks. In real life, you lose people, they stay lost. The galaxy doesn't bring them back to you. Your precious Force doesn't make the galaxy any less empty."

"It's less empty now," Ferus said. "Now that the Force has brought you back to me. And me back to you."

Div snorted. "And what good is that? We're both broken, Ferus. Or haven't you noticed?"

"The Force doesn't always give us what we want, or even what we need," Ferus said. "But it always gives us something we can use. To survive."

"And that's exactly what we do," Div said bitterly. "Survive. Good for us."

"Yes, Lune."

Div didn't correct the name. And when Ferus put a hand on his shoulder, Div didn't shrug him off. Ferus smiled sadly. "Good for us."

The garrison was burning, a towering inferno that set the horizon ablaze. The stormtroopers in the surrounding hills had abandoned their fight with the Rebels and were doing their best to combat the flames. But it was no use. Slowly but surely, the garrison was crumbling to the ground. It was just one building — but it was enough to spark a fire in the heart of every Belazuran who chafed at Imperial control.

As word of the successful attack spread around the city, the Belazurans remembered what it had been like ten years before, when they'd still had the will to fight. And as they remembered, their courage returned to them. They laid down their fusioncutters and their servodrivers. They stepped away from their assembly lines of Imperial weapons. Some took to the streets, throwing rocks at their Imperial guards or slamming furniture through the windows of Imperial quarters. Others lit a match. And smoke choked the sky.

As day dropped into night, Luke stood on the hill, watching it happen. Watching a city reclaim its soul. The Empire would fight back; it always did. And maybe it would destroy this uprising as it had destroyed the others.

But as the factories burned and the skies glowed with reflected flames, Luke couldn't help hoping — that this time, the fire would last.

oresh cut off the transmission. So it was over. The garrison was destroyed. X-7 was dead. The ambush was a failure, and the entire city was in upheaval. And Soresh, as the highest-ranking officer on the planet, would be the one held responsible. "No," he said quietly, shaking his head. "No, no, no. *No.*" He smashed a fist down on the desk, scattering piles of flimsiplast everywhere. This was *not* the way it was supposed to go. He was a loyal servant of the Empire. The *most* loyal. Hadn't he sacrificed everything for the cause? Years of his life. His family. Even his own son.

After such devotion and such sacrifice, all for the greater glory of the Empire, surely Palpatine would understand.

Everyone made mistakes.

Still, it couldn't hurt to put as much distance between himself and this disaster as possible. He slipped his private datapad into his pocket and hurried to the door. But when it swung open, a stormtrooper was blocking his path. "I'll need you to prepare the ship," he said. "I'm leaving immediately."

The stormtrooper raised his blaster. "I'm sorry, sir, but that's not possible."

"Not possible? What do you mean? Is something wrong with the ship? I'll take another. Surely this planet must have a ship!" Soresh realized he was starting to sound hysterical, and forced himself to take a deep breath. "Let me by," he said in a more commanding voice. "That's an order."

"You're to stay here until he arrives," the stormtrooper said in that flat, toneless voice they all used.

"Until who arrives?" Soresh asked, not sure he wanted the answer.

"Lord Vader."

No.

He assumed a military posture, shoulders back, chest out, head held high. "Listen to me. I don't know who you are, but *I* am Commander Rezi Soresh, Imperial sub-overseer of strategic and tactical operations, with dominion over the Inner Rim and all planets contained within. You take orders from me, not Lord Vader. And I'm ordering you to let me pass."

The stormtrooper didn't move. Soresh fumed. It was pointless to reason with these stormtroopers. Hiding behind that implacable mask, they had no need to be human. Sometimes, when he stared into that white plastoid armor, it was hard to believe that there even was a real person beneath it. And who knew what lay behind the mask? It could be a man, could be a woman, could be a cold-blooded monster.

Like Vader. No one knew what was behind that black faceplate, but Soresh was certain that whatever it was contained no shred of humanity. Or mercy.

He stepped back into the office and slammed the door, then locked it. He was running out of time.

Soresh had never considered himself the kind of man who would make a fatal mistake. But he *was* the kind of man who planned for every eventuality, even the unlikeliest ones. Which meant he never went anywhere without a backup plan.

Darth Vader spoke for the Emperor. For Soresh to disobey a direct order would mean violating his sacred oath. By fleeing, he would become an enemy of everything he believed in.

But staying meant certain death. And if he survived, he could atone. He could show the Emperor how loyal he was. How valuable. He could find some way to prove he deserved to live.

If he survived.

Soresh pressed the button that swung back the bookshelf and revealed the hidden turbolift. The secret Rebel escape route was the reason he had selected the office for his temporary quarters. Those Belazuran Rebels had apparently been very crafty when it came to surviving. *Not crafty enough,* Soresh thought, and their loss was his gain. The lift was still operational, which meant Vader didn't know about it. Soresh himself knew only because he had done his research and studied the blueprints, as he studied the blueprints of every building he planned to spend significant time in.

And he never arrived on a planet without making sure that he had an alternate way to depart. In this case, it was an old CloakShape fighter stashed in a secure location.

Like all the bullies Soresh had faced over the years, Vader was stronger than him. Bolder. More powerful in every way. Guaranteed to triumph in any face-to-face confrontation. But, like all the other bullies, Vader had overlooked one very important fact.

Soresh was smarter.

It was all the advantage he would need.

"Mug of lum for your thoughts, kid?" Han asked, joining Luke at the galley's small table. He slid a foaming glass toward Luke, but Luke waved it away. Han shook his head, then gulped it down himself, draining the glass in two swallows. "You look like you could use some distraction."

"I could use some *privacy*," Luke muttered, but he

wasn't about to get that any time soon. The *Millennium Falcon* was full to capacity, and more. Five humans, two droids, and a Wookiee were proving to be more than even the *Falcon* could handle. At least as far as Luke was concerned. But maybe that was just because he was stuck sharing his bunk with Div and Ferus. Div's permanent glower made it clear that he would rather be somewhere — anywhere else. And Ferus . . . well, Luke trusted him, even liked him, but there was something uncomfortably intense about the man's stare. It was like he could see right through to the center of Luke — and was judging whether Luke was worthy.

Worthy of what, Luke didn't know.

"Smile, kid," Han recommended. "The good guys won, the bad guys are two meters under. Not bad for a day's work, eh?"

"Not bad," Luke agreed, but his heart wasn't in it.

X-7 was dead. The man who'd betrayed him, who'd tried to kill him again and again was gone. And a major Imperial base was gone with him. Han was right, it was time to celebrate. Not to stare moodily into space, as he'd been doing for the last several hours.

"So what is it?" Han asked. He leaned back in his chair and kicked his feet up on the table. Luke wondered how it would feel to be Han, to float through life without a care in the world. No ties, no responsibilities, no burdens — no fear.

Luke couldn't imagine.

He shrugged. "I'm just wondering what's next."

"Next?" Han grinned. "Next we get ourselves back to Yavin 4 and breathe some nice, clean, Imperial-free air. We stop looking over our shoulders wondering when some crazy assassin's going to shoot you from behind a tree. And I wouldn't mind a nice big juicy nerf steak while we're at it."

"I mean after that," Luke explained. "X-7's not the end of it. There's never an end of it." There never would be, not until the Empire had fallen. Life had become one battle after another, one death after another. He had told himself that something would change once X-7 was dead.

He was tired.

"You can't think about that kind of thing," Han said. "Forget about what might happen, and —"

"Easy for you to say!" Luke exploded. "*Everything's* easy for you. But some of us actually care about the Rebellion, and about . . . other people," he finished lamely, reluctant to name names. "We can't just dash off to some other part of the galaxy when things don't go our way."

Han stood up, his face red. "Listen, kid, I don't know who you've been talking to, but nothing about my life is *easy*. And if you weren't such a —" He stopped himself and drew in a deep breath. "You know the difference between you and me, kid?"

Luke sighed. "I'm sure you're going to tell me."

Han slapped Luke on the back. Hard. "Right you are." He sat down again. "You think I've got nothing on my mind? I'll tell you what I've got: a bounty on my head worth more credits than you'll see in your entire life. Not to mention a very angry Hutt who probably wants me skinned alive and hung on his trophy wall. Trust me, kid, I got troubles. But the difference between you and me is that I know when to forget about them. You're right, something *always* happens next — and it's never something good. But it's going to happen whether you worry about it or not. So when you get a day like this, everything actually going right and no one trying to kill you? Better enjoy it while it lasts, that's what I say."

"You may be right," Luke admitted.

"Always am," Han pointed out. "Don't see why now should be any different."

Han had a point. So when Leia and Ferus joined them in the galley for food and drink, Luke joined into the festivities. When C-3PO and R2-D2 started bickering and Chewbacca threatened to rip their gears out if they didn't quiet down, Luke laughed along with everyone else. But his smile was strained.

Somewhere out there in the dark, something was waiting.

Waiting for me, Luke thought, uneasy.

Coming for me.

When he turned back to the group, Ferus was watching him, as usual. Something about the older man's expression convinced him: Ferus felt it, too.

But Han was right, there was nothing to be done about it . . . now. Luke tried his best to shake off the dark cloud. Whatever came next, he would face it. *They* would face it, together. And in the meantime, he had his friends, he had his moment of triumph — and peace.

So maybe he would do exactly as Han said.

Enjoy it while it lasts.

Darth Vader swept down the hallway, his cape flowing behind him. Stormtroopers lined the corridor, shrinking away as he passed. The stench of fear oozed out of them, and Vader breathed it in greedily. Their terror made him stronger, gave power to the dark Force within him. Another day, he might have paused to toy with them. Strike one down and watch the rest scatter like fearful sand skitters. But this was not the time for games.

A man had dared to defy him; that man would be destroyed.

He threw open the doors of Soresh's chamber. But there was no one there but a young lieutenant, rifling through the sheets of flimsiplast strewn across the desk. "Where is he?" Vader said, anger percolating deep within.

The man trembled. "He . . . h-he . . . We don't know,

my lord," he stammered. "He was here, but now . . ."

"You were ordered to hold him for my arrival," Vader said.

"We stationed guards, but . . ." The man shook his head. His face was drained of color. He was young, little more than a boy. This was probably his first assignment.

"But *he is gone!*" Vader roared, and let the anger overtake him. The boy's eyes bulged. His face flushed red. His hands crept to his neck. His mouth fell open, his tongue hanging out like that of a hungry massiff.

Vader boiled. *Defied,* by a coward like Rezi Soresh. Because of the sheer incompetence of those who served him. It was an *insult,* an *offense.* It could not be allowed. He let the dark side flow through him, let its shadow fill the room with its enormous power. He nurtured the anger, feeding it, feeling it swell within him.

The boy gasped. One last breath.

And then he dropped to the ground, eyes open, chest still.

The rage quieted. Vader was satisfied. For the moment.

But Soresh was still out there, willfully defying him, and perhaps still pursuing the Rebel Luke Skywalker, even though it had been expressly forbidden. Vader would find him, stop him.

But first Vader would punish him.

He spread his consciousness out into the corners of

the room, letting it merge with the Force, exploring this pathetic world with its prying tendrils, searching for some hint to where Soresh might have gone. But it wasn't Soresh that he sensed. It was something else — something familiar. He had felt it several times these last few months, but always faintly. He hadn't been sure. But now he was.

The past tickled at the edges of his mind. He had felt this presence before, long ago. Then he had been weak, still afraid to face what he had become. Still imprisoned by the memories of Anakin Skywalker.

No more. The past held no danger for him, not anymore. Facing Obi-Wan Kenobi had been deeply satisfying, knowing he had extinguished his light forever. There was only one other man in the galaxy whose death would give him as much satisfaction. For years, Vader had assumed he was already dead. But now . . .

Behind his mask, Vader drew his lips back in a predatory smile.

It's been a long time, old friend, he thought. *Too long. See you soon.*